Carol Marinelli is a rising star
of Harlequin Presents®, and we hope
that you'll continue to enjoy her stories
in the months and years to come.
Carol's intense, dramatic and
passionate romances will take you
on a roller coaster of emotions!

The Billionaire's Contract Bride
is a sensual story, jam-packed with
excitement and instinctive desire....

THE AUSTRALIANS

Where spirited women win the hearts of
Australia's most eligible men!

Look for the next exciting story in this series,
written by fan-favorite author Miranda Lee.

Coming June 2004:

The Passion Price
#2398

Available only from Harlequin Presents®

Carol Marinelli

THE BILLIONAIRE'S CONTRACT BRIDE

THE AUSTRALIANS

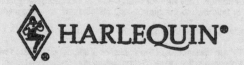

HARLEQUIN®

TORONTO • NEW YORK • LONDON
AMSTERDAM • PARIS • SYDNEY • HAMBURG
STOCKHOLM • ATHENS • TOKYO • MILAN • MADRID
PRAGUE • WARSAW • BUDAPEST • AUCKLAND

For Mario
With love and gratitude for all your support
Carol

ISBN 0-373-12372-8

THE BILLIONAIRE'S CONTRACT BRIDE

First North American Publication 2004.

Copyright © 2003 by Carol Marinelli.

This edition published by arrangement with Harlequin Books S.A.

Visit us at www.eHarlequin.com

Printed in U.S.A.

CHAPTER ONE

'THEY'RE never going to believe us.' Taking Aiden's hand, Tabitha stepped out of the car, her mouth literally dropping open as she watched the guests milling on the steps of the grand old Melbourne church like a parade of shimmering peacocks.

'Why ever not?' Aiden didn't look remotely fazed, waving cheerfully to a couple of familiar faces in the crowd.

'They're never going to believe us,' Tabitha repeated, after taking a deep steadying breath, 'because I don't look like a society wife.'

'Thank God,' Aiden muttered. 'Anyway, you're not a society wife; you're merely pretending to be my girlfriend. So if it's any consolation, you're allowed to have sex appeal. They'll think you're my last wild fling before I finally settle down.'

'They'll see through it straight away,' Tabitha argued, refusing to believe it could all be so simple. 'I'm a dancer, Aiden, not an actress. Why on earth did I agree to this?'

'You had no choice,' Aiden reminded her, before she could bolt back into the car. They started to walk, albeit slowly, towards the gathering throng. 'I played the part of your devoted fiancé at your school reunion in return for you accompanying me to my cousin's wedding. Simple.'

'No,' Tabitha said, pulling Aiden's hand so he had to slow down. 'Simple would be telling your family that

5

you're gay. It's the twenty-first century, for heaven's sake; it's not a crime any more!'

'Try telling that to my father. Honestly, Tabitha, it's better this way, and don't worry for a second about not looking the part—you look fabulous.'

'Courtesy of your credit card,' Tabitha scolded. 'You shouldn't have spent all that money, Aiden.'

'Cheap at half the price; anyway, I wouldn't dream of throwing you into the snake pit that is my family without a designer frock and shoes. Oh, come on, Tabitha, enjoy yourself. You love a good wedding!'

After slipping into the pew and idly scanning the Order of Service, Tabitha let her jade eyes work the congregation, and though it galled her to admit it she had never been more grateful for the small fortune that had been spent on her outfit. What had seemed appropriate for the multitude of weddings she had attended this year definitely wouldn't have done today.

Her dress had been a true find, the flimsy chiffon fabric a near perfect match for her Titian hair, which she wore today pinned back from her face but cascading around her shoulders. Her lips and nails were painted a vibrant coral that matched her impossibly high strappy sandals and beaded bag perfectly, and Tabitha felt a million dollars. It was a colour scheme Tabitha would normally never even have considered, with her long red curls and pale skin, yet for once the gushing sales assistant hadn't been lying: it all went beautifully.

The guests that packed the church seemed to ooze money and style—for the most part, at least. But there were more than a couple of garish fashion mistakes to giggle over that even Tabitha recognised—born, she assumed, from a bottomless wallet and an utter disregard

for taste. Aiden took great delight in pointing out each
and every one, rather too loudly.

An incredibly tall woman with the widest hat imaginable chose to sit directly in front of Tabitha, which
ruined any hope of a decent view of the proceedings.
But even with Aiden's and Tabitha's combined critical
eyes there wasn't even a hint of a fashion *faux pas* in
sight on this ravishing creature. Height obviously didn't
bother this woman either, judging by the razor-sharp sti-
lettos strapped to her slender feet. Oh, well, Tabitha
shrugged, it must be nice to have so much confidence.

Only when the woman turned to watch the bridal procession did Tabitha start with recognition. Amy Dellier
was one of the top models in Australia, and, judging by
the extremely favourable write-ups in all the glossies
Tabitha devotedly devoured, she was all set for inter-
national fame. Suddenly the golden chiffon and coral
which she had been so pleased with only a few moments
ago seemed a rather paltry offering, standing so close to
this stunning woman.

As the organ thundered into the 'Bridal March' they
all stood, every eye turning as the bride entered and
started her slow walk down the aisle. Every eye, that
was, except Tabitha's. She had seen more brides this
summer than a wedding photographer. Instead, some
morbid fascination found her gaze constantly straying to
Amy Dellier. She truly was beautiful—stunningly so.
Not a line or blemish marred her perfect complexion,
and her make-up highlighted the vivid aquamarine of her
eyes.

'Excuse me.' A deep voice dragged her back to the
proceedings. 'I need to get past.'

The voice was deep and sensual, and as she turned
her head Tabitha almost braced herself for disappoint-

ment. It probably belonged to some portly fifty-year-old who did voice-over commercials part-time. But there was nothing disappointing about the face that met hers. If Amy Dellier was the epitome of feminine perfection, then standing before Tabitha was the male version. Jet hair was brushed back from a strong haughty face, and high cheekbones forced her attention to the darkest eyes she had ever seen. At first glance they seemed black, but closer inspection revealed a deep indigo, framed with thick black spiky eyelashes. The heady scent of his cologne and his immaculate grooming indicated he was freshly shaven, but the dusky shadow on his strong jaw conjured images of bandanas and tequila, a world away from the sharp expensive suit he was wearing. He looked sultry and masculine—animal, in fact. As if no amount of grooming, money or trappings could ever take away the earthy, primal essence of man.

'Of course.' Swallowing nervously, she pushed her legs back against the pew in an attempt to let him past—but her bag was blocking the way, with Aiden's foot on the strap. Aiden, totally mesmerised by the wedding, was happily oblivious to the obstruction he was causing.

'Sorry.' His apology was mere politeness, exactly as one would expect when a stranger had to push past—the same as at the movies, when the inevitable hordes returned with their dripping ice-creams and you had to lift your legs up and squash back into the seat to let them past. Except demi-gods like this never appeared at the movies Tabitha attended—at least not off screen—and this moment seemed to be going on for ever.

If he didn't want to fall, he had no choice but to steady himself briefly on Tabitha's bare arm as he stepped over the small bag. The pews were impossibly close, each jammed to capacity with guests. As his hand touched the flesh of her arm Tabitha found she was holding her breath; two spots of colour flamed on her carefully rouged cheeks as he brushed past her, the scent of him filling her nostrils.

Aiden turned then, a smile of recognition on his face as he mouthed hello to this delicious stranger. The bride was passing, and he had no choice but to stand between Tabitha and Aiden as the procession slowly passed.

So slowly.

It was probably only a matter of seconds.

It seemed to last for ever.

Never had she felt such awareness—the whole focus of her attention honing in on this everyday occurrence. Her skin was stinging as she stood next to him, every nerve in her being standing rigid to attention, so painfully aware of his close proximity. But all too soon it was over; the procession had dutifully passed, allowing him to slip into the pew in front and Tabitha to finally breathe again.

He moved directly into the seat reserved next to Amy, and by the way her hand coiled possessively around his she was only too pleased to see him.

Tabitha found herself letting out a disappointed sigh while simultaneously admonishing herself for overreacting. Well, what did you expect? she reasoned. That someone as utterly gorgeous as that would be here alone?

Only she wasn't talking about Amy Dellier.

'Dearly beloved...'

The congregation hushed as the service started, but it held no interest for Tabitha. Instead her attention was entirely focused on the delicious sight of the man who had sat himself in front of her. His thick hair was beautifully cut and absolutely black, without even a single grey hair. It sharply tapered into a thick, strong and tanned neck, and his suit was superbly cut over his wide shoulders. As they stood to sing the first hymn Tabitha stared, mesmerised, her eyes unashamedly flicking downward. Despite her height, Amy Dellier seemed almost petite beside her partner; he was incredibly tall. It was no wonder she could get away wearing heels with him around.

'Don't even think about it,' Aiden whispered into her ear as the congregation sang heartily.

'What are you talking about?' Tabitha flushed, snapping her attention to the hymn book she was holding in front of her.

It didn't work. 'You're supposed to be on page forty-five, Tab.' Aiden grinned. 'That, my dear, is my brother Zavier.'

'I don't know who you're talking about.'

But Aiden had known her far too long to be fobbed off. 'You know exactly who I'm talking about, Tabitha, and take it from me—he'd crush you in the palm of his hand.'

Tabitha winced at the expression. 'Meaning?'

'Just that. Zavier might be a dream to look at, but he's bad news.'

Their heads were huddled over the hymn book, and they spoke out of the sides of their mouths, but it wasn't enough to prevent a few withering looks being cast in their direction. 'Then it's just as well I'm not interested,' Tabitha hissed.

Aiden gave her a knowing look. 'On your head be it, but don't say I didn't warn you.'

She sang tunelessly, her eyes straying all too often to the delectable diversion so achingly close in front of her. Despite her recent aversion to weddings, this one was turning out to be a sheer pleasure; even the endless wait while the happy couple went off to sign the register passed in a blur of delicious fantasy. Never had she felt such a strong physical attraction to someone—someone she knew absolutely nothing about. He was completely unattainable, of course. Way, way out of her league.

Despite her protests, Tabitha had to admit that hob-nobbing with the seriously rich had its perks. There was no question of standing bored and thirsty as the photographer clicked away for hours. Instead, a small marquee had been set up in Melbourne's Botanical Gardens and delicious fruit and champagne were being served as the family mingled, disappearing when the photographer called them to do their duty.

Accepting a glass of champagne, Tabitha smiled as she was introduced to Aiden's parents. Despite Aiden's gloomy descriptions, Tabitha was instantly won over and utterly in awe of Aidan's mother, Marjory, who oozed glamour and wealth.

'A lovely wedding, wasn't it? Though I'm not sure Simone's dress was quite the part. I really don't think thigh-length splits are appropriate attire in a church. What did you think, Jeremy darling?'

Jeremy Chambers had none of his wife's effervescence. His black eyes were as guarded as Zavier's, his haughty face as stern and unyielding as his favourite son's. 'She looked like any of the other brides I've seen this year,' he answered loudly, not remotely bothered who overheard him.

'I know the feeling,' Tabitha groaned, then instantly regretted her comment. 'I've been to rather too many weddings myself this summer,' she offered by way of explanation, taking a good slurp of her champagne. As

Jeremy's stern gaze turned to her she wished that she'd stayed quiet, but Jeremy actually smiled.

'Tell me about it,' he said gloomily. 'How many have you been to?'

'Ten,' Tabitha exaggerated, then did a quick mental calculation. 'Well, six, at the very least,' she added, rolling her eyes. 'All my friends seem to have taken the plunge *en masse*.'

'That's just the start of it,' Jeremy said knowingly. 'The next few years will be taken up with christenings, and before you know where you are all your friends' children are getting married and the whole merry-go-round starts again. Marjory loves weddings, unlike me, and feels duty-bound to attend each and every one—no matter how distant the relative. Speaking of which, I'd best go and say hello to a few. It was a pleasure meeting you, Tabitha.' He went to shake her hand, but halfway there seemed to change his mind and instead kissed her on the cheek, much to Aiden's wide-eyed amazement.

'My goodness, you've actually made a hit—my father doesn't usually like *anyone*.'

'He seems charming,' Tabitha scolded. 'I can't believe all the awful things you've said about him.'

'He is charming, if you happen to be the right son—and talk of the devil...'

'Zavier!' Marjory exclaimed, kissing him warmly on the cheek. 'I thought you weren't ever going to make it to the church. Where on earth did you get to?'

'Where do you think I got to?' Tabitha noticed his haughty demeanour was somewhat softened when he addressed his mother. 'I was working.'

'But it's Saturday,' Marjory protested. 'Not that that ever stopped you, Zavier. But that's quite enough about work—I, for one, intend to enjoy myself today. Have you met Tabitha, Aiden's darling, er...' the pause was interminable, but Marjory eventually recovered. '...er, friend?'

Aiden took a hefty swig of his drink, avoiding Tabitha's eyes. Only Zavier's gaze stayed steadily trained on her.

'Briefly, in the church.' He offered his hand and she shook it gingerly, noticing how hot and strong his grip was.

'Where's Lucy?' Marjory asked.

'*Amy,*' Zavier corrected, 'is touching up her make-up.'

'Lovely girl,' Marjory said warmly. 'She'd make a beautiful bride.'

'Subtle as a brick, as always,' Zavier groaned.

'Well, what choice do I have? I've got two sons in their thirties,' she said, her eyes on Tabitha, 'and not even the tiniest hint at a wedding, let alone grandchildren. Simone's barely twenty; no wonder Carmella's grinning from ear to ear.'

'The reason she's grinning is because Simone's actually managed to nab someone rich enough to get them out of debt—not because of her daughter's eternal happiness.'

'Ahh!' Marjory wagged a playful finger. 'Being out of debt practically ensures eternal happiness.'

'For you, perhaps,' Zavier quipped. 'Anyway, given that you can't even get Amy's name right, I think that says a lot for your motives. Forget it.'

'It would make your father so proud.'

Tabitha was actually enjoying the conversation. She liked the gentle verbal sparring between mother and son, and even Zavier didn't seem so formidable up against the feisty Marjory. But as she mentioned his father suddenly the temperature seemed to drop, and the affectionate, teasing reply that Tabitha eagerly awaited never came. Zavier Chambers, the epitome of confidence, suddenly seemed lost for words.

'It *would*, Zavier,' Marjory said, a note of urgency in her voice. 'It's your father's dearest wish.'

'What's your father's dearest wish?' All eyes turned as Amy appeared. Immaculate, gorgeous, wafting expensive perfume, she sidled up to Zavier and wrapped her arm around him. But Zavier barely acknowledged her presence. 'What did I miss, darling?' Amy persisted in a low, throaty purr.

'Nothing,' Zavier said darkly, shooting his mother a warning look. 'At least nothing that you have to worry about, Amy.' And, extracting himself from her clutches, he nodded to the photographer who was hovering on the sidelines. 'I think we're wanted.'

Even though she had just checked her make-up, Amy whipped out a mirror from her bag and started dabbing at her lips.

'Come on, Tabitha.' Aiden beckoned, but Tabitha shook her head.

'You go. I'm hardly family.'

'What's that got to do with it? Come on.'

But Tabitha was insistent. Immortalising a lie seemed wrong, somehow. 'The photographer said family only. Please, Aiden, don't make me feel any worse about this.'

'You'll be all right on your own for five minutes?'

'For heaven's sake, Aiden, just go. They're all waiting.'

Sipping on her drink, she watched as they all lined up; it was easy to tell which side they all belonged to. The Chamberses reminded Tabitha of a Mafia movie— all their suits seemed darker, all the men taller, all their hair cut just that little bit more neatly. The fatal combination of money and a perfect gene pool—only Aiden didn't quite fit in with the masses. His features were gentler, his gestures more expressive than the tight-lipped brooding looks of his relatives. Zavier stood out also. If the Chambers family were a formidable bunch then Zavier was the pinnacle—taller, darker, and, from the reverent way everyone treated him, the most powerful.

'So you've been relegated to the role of bystander as well?'

Startled, Tabitha turned, only then registering that Amy wasn't up there amongst them.

'It's a bit early in the piece for me to start appearing in family albums,' Tabitha said lightly, somewhat taken aback that someone so famous was actually talking to her.

'And a bit late in the piece for me; I think I've just been dumped.'

'Oh.'

'Bloody Chambers.' The sob in Amy's voice was one of raw anguish, and Tabitha watched, startled, as tears slid down the oh-so famous face. With a strangled cry she attempted to run off, but soft grass combined with six-inch heels didn't make for a dignified exit, and Tabitha cringed as she watched her trip away.

'It's the effect I have on women,' Zavier quipped as he joined Tabitha. 'They can't get away quickly enough.'

'What on earth did you say to her?' Tabitha asked, even though she knew it was none of her business.

'Not much. I just pointed out it was pretty stupid for her to be in the family photo when she wasn't going to be around long enough for the films to be developed.'

'But that's horrible,' Tabitha gasped. 'Couldn't you have finished with her in a nicer way?'

Zavier shrugged. 'Believe me, I tried. Unfortunately she either didn't want to hear it, or it was beyond her comprehension that a man actually might not want her.'

Tabitha stole a closer look, and knew it must be the former. Zavier had a haughty, effortless arrogance that must be a natural by-product when you were so beautiful. And beautiful just about summed him up: an immaculate prototype that left all others as a pale comparison. No wonder Amy hadn't wanted to hear it was over. To have known such perfection, no matter how briefly, would ensure a lifetime addiction.

He didn't seem remotely bothered by her scrutiny, and calmly stood as Tabitha surveyed him. Only when she realised the pause had gone on far too long and that she was obviously staring did Tabitha flush, instantly snapping back to the conversation in hand. She was cross at herself for being caught unguarded, and the scorn in her voice came easily. Gorgeous he might be, but beauty was only skin-deep, and it would serve her well to remember that fact.

'Well, I think you treated her appallingly.'

He raised an eyebrow. 'My, you do get worked up easily, don't you? I assume that hair colour didn't come out of a bottle, then?' Picking up a mass of curls, he pretended to examine them as Tabitha stood burning with indignation. Suddenly he was close, far too close for comfort, the dark pools of his eyes so near she could see the tiny sapphire flecks in them.

'Of course it didn't.' Flicking his hand away, she felt her hair tumble down over her shoulders. The brush of his hand on hers was electric, and she felt a blush stealing across her chest, working its way up her long, slen-

der neck to meet with the scorching heat of her cheeks.
'I don't know why any woman would put up with you.'

'I can answer that for you.'

Tabitha shook her head angrily. 'It wasn't a question;
it was a statement. Just because you're rich and good-
looking you think you can treat women…' Her voice
tailed off as she realised he was laughing—laughing at
her.

'So I'm good-looking, am I?'

Tabitha snorted and instantly regretted it; the undig-
nified noise hardly did her gorgeous frock justice. 'You
know you are, and you think that gives you a licence to
hurt people.'

'Considering we only met…' he glanced at the heavy
gold watch on his wrist, his eyes narrowing slightly as
he did so '…an hour ago, you seem to have formed a
rather hasty opinion, and from the venom in your voice
I'm assuming it's not a good one. Can I ask why?'

She stood there, searching for an answer. Why had
her reaction to him been so violent? Why was she angry
at him for so carelessly discarding Amy when if the truth
were known Tabitha knew nothing about the circumstances that had led to the conclusion of their relationship? 'I just don't like seeing people hurt,' she said finally, while knowing her response was woefully
inadequate.

'Amy's not hurt,' he answered irritably. 'She got exactly what she wanted from me: her picture in all the
social pages and a fast ticket to fame. As for rich and
good-looking—I don't think she has any trouble quali-
fying for that title either.'

'She *was* hurt,' Tabitha insisted, but Zavier just
shrugged nonchalantly.

'Maybe,' Zavier conceded, but any surge of triumph

for Tabitha was quickly quashed when he carried on talking, a wry smile tugging at the corner of his full sensual mouth. 'After all, she's just lost the best lover she's ever had.'

'You're disgusting,' Tabitha spluttered, her cheeks flaming as her mind danced with the dangerous images that had suddenly flooded her mind.

'Just truthful. Look, we had a good time while it lasted. Amy wanted more, and I wasn't prepared to give it to her.' He gave a dry laugh. 'The grass is a bit damp here to go down on bended knee.'

'She wanted to get married?'

Zavier nodded.

'But that's even worse.' Tabitha was genuinely appalled. 'She loves you and you ended it like that?'

But Zavier just shook his head. 'Who said anything about love?' He saw the confusion in her eyes and it seemed to amuse him. 'You think Amy loved me?'

'Why else would she want to marry you?'

'Oh, come on, Tabitha—surely you're not that naïve? For the same reason that you're here with my brother: money and position. Why let a little detail like love get in the way of a good deal?'

'But I'm not with Aiden for his money.' She was stunned that he thought this of her.

'Please,' he scoffed.

'I'm not,' she retorted furiously, but Zavier wasn't listening.

'Sorry I took so long, Mr Chambers.' A waitress rushed over, a glass of ice and a bottle of mineral water in her hand.

'Just the bottle will do.' He took a long drink as Tabitha searched frantically for Aiden. Finally catching sight of him, Tabitha groaned inwardly. The bride was chattering to him now, which meant there was no chance of imminent rescue; she'd just have to make the best of it.

'So what do you do?'

'Excuse me?'

'For a living.' Her patience was starting to run out now. 'I mean, I assume that you work?'

His brow furrowed for a moment before he answered. 'I work in the family business; I would have thought you'd have at least known that.'

Tabitha frowned; there was obviously rather a lot of ground that she hadn't covered with Aiden, and his brother's resumé was one of them. Still, she was happy to attempt a recovery. 'That's right! Aiden did mention it, of course. I'm useless with names and details like that.'

'So how did you meet my brother?'

'At a party.'

'Well, it wouldn't have been at work, would it?' He flashed a very dry, guarded smile. 'We both know the effect that four-letter word has on my brother.'

'Aiden does work,' Tabitha bit back. 'He's a very talented artist.'

'Oh, he's an artist all right.' Zavier's black eyes worked the crowd and they both watched as Aiden knocked back one drink, grabbing a couple more from the passing waiter. 'Dedicated too,' Zavier mused. 'So, what do you do for a living?'

Tabitha swallowed. Normally she loved saying what she did for a living, loved the response it evoked in people, but somehow she couldn't quite imagine Zavier's face lighting up with undisguised admiration when she revealed her chosen profession. 'I dance.'

He didn't say a word, not a single word, but his eyes

spoke volumes as they slowly travelled her body, one quizzical eyebrow raised in a curiously mocking gesture as she blushed under his scrutiny.

'Not that type of dancing,' she flared. 'I work on the stage.'

'Classical?' he asked, in the snobbiest most derisive of tones.

'A—a bit,' Tabitha stammered. 'But mainly modern. Every now and then I even get to do a poor man's version of the Can-Can.' The bitter edge to her voice was obvious, even to herself, and she blinked in surprise at her own admission.

A sliver of a smile moved his lips a fraction and his eyes languorously drifted the length of her long legs. 'Is that the sound of a frustrated leading lady I hear?'

'Possibly.' Tabitha shrugged. Hell, why was she feeling like this? Why did one withering stare from him reduce her to a showgirl? 'But, for your information, I'm actually very good at what I do,' Tabitha flared. 'You might mock what your brother and I do for a living, but you don't have to pull on a suit to put in an honest day's work. We happen to give a lot of people a lot of pleasure.'

'Oh, I'm sure you do.' Again those black eyes worked her body, and again Tabitha mentally kicked herself at the opening she had given him.

For something to do Tabitha drained her glass and accepted another from a passing waiter. But still Zavier's black eyes stayed trained on her, making even the most basic task, such as breathing, seem suddenly terribly complicated.

'Don't worry.' He smiled at her for the first time, but just as Tabitha felt herself relax his cutting voice set the hairs on the back of her neck standing to attention. 'I mean, once you get that ring on your finger you'll be able to hang up your dancing shoes for ever.'

Her jade eyes flashed with anger at his inference. 'I'll have you know that I happen to enjoy my job—very much, in fact. If you really think I'm seeing Aiden for the chance to marry into his charming family—' she flashed a wry smile '—you couldn't be more wrong.'

Her fiery response to his provocative statement did nothing to mar his smooth expression, and he stood there irritatingly calm as Tabitha flushed with anger.

'We'll see,' he said darkly. 'But something tells me I'm not going to be pleasantly surprised.'

Aiden appeared then, oblivious of the simmering tension. 'Glad to see you're getting along.' He smiled warmly. 'Isn't she gorgeous, Zavier?' He squeezed Tabitha around the waist as he haphazardly deposited a kiss on her cheek.

'Gorgeous,' Zavier quipped, his smile belying the menacing look in his eyes. 'Now, if you two will excuse me?' He flashed the briefest of nods vaguely in her direction as Tabitha stood there mute. 'It was a pleasure meeting you.'

Not a pleasure, exactly, Tabitha mused as he walked away, but it had certainly been an experience; the only trouble was, she couldn't quite decide whether it was one that she wanted to repeat.

CHAPTER TWO

THE meal seemed to go on for ever, the speeches even longer. Tabitha spent most of the time smarting over Zavier's comments, pushing her food around her plate and drinking rather too much. She hated Zavier Chambers for his cruel suggestion that she was some sort of gold-digger when the actual truth was she was doing his damn family a favour: saving Jeremy Chambers from the news he didn't want to hear.

Aiden was unusually on edge—an inevitable by-product, Tabitha guessed, of being in such close proximity to his family. His promise to stay by her side all night diminished with each drink he consumed, and rather too much of the night was spent sitting like the proverbial wallflower as Aiden worked the room, only returning to reclaim his glass every now and then.

'Go easy, Aiden,' Tabitha said as Aiden knocked back yet another drink.

'I need a few drinks under my belt to face this lot.' He gave her an apologetic grin. 'Sorry, I'm not being very good company, am I? They just set my teeth on edge. How are you finding it?'

Tabitha shrugged. 'Not bad, but then I've only got to deal with it for tonight. I didn't realise your family was so well heeled—I mean, from what you'd told me I'd guessed that they were wealthy, of course, but nothing like this. You should have warned me.' She gestured to the room.

The Windsor Hotel was Melbourne's finest, and the ballroom where the wedding reception was being held was quite simply breathtaking. Everything was divine, from the icy cold champagne and the canapés that had been served as they entered, to the lavish banquet they were now finishing up.

'Why would I do that? I had enough trouble getting you to come in the first place. If you'd known it was going to be like this wild horses wouldn't have dragged you here.'

Aiden was right, of course. Here amongst Australia's élite, with vintage champagne flowing like water, Tabitha felt way out of her depth.

Aiden hiccoughed softly, staring moodily into his drink. 'Tab?' he said gently. 'What's the matter tonight? And before you say "nothing", just remember that we've been friends too long to pretend everything's all right when it clearly isn't. It's not just the wedding that's upsetting you, is it? What's going on?'

She didn't answer, her long fingers toying with her red curls, coiling them around her fingers in an almost child-like manner.

'Is it your grandmother?' As she bit into her lip Aiden knew he'd hit the mark. 'What's she done now?' There was a touch of humour in his voice as he tried to lighten the mood and cajole the problem out of her. 'Sold the family jewels?'

Tabitha's eyes weren't smiling as she looked up. 'My family's not like yours, Aiden; we don't have "family jewels". Sorry,' she added, 'this isn't your fault.'

'What isn't? Come on, Tab, tell me what's going on.'

'She remortgaged her house.' Tabitha let out the long breath she had inadvertently been holding. 'To pay off all her gambling debts.'

'You already told me that—last month, if I remember rightly,' Aiden pointed out. 'You went to the bank with her and helped organize it. Can't she manage the repayments?'

'She withdrew the loan,' Tabitha started in an unusually shaky voice, 'and promptly fed it back into the poker machines at the casino.'

'All of it?'

Aiden's open mouth and wide eyes weren't exactly helping, and Tabitha nodded glumly. 'So now she's got all the old debts that were causing so many problems plus a massive new one, and it's all my fault.'

'How on earth do you work that one out?'

'I shouldn't have left her with access to so much money. She's like a moth to a flame where the casino's concerned; I don't even think it's the gambling she's addicted to, more the company. I should have made her pay off her bills...'

'She's not a child,' Aiden pointed out, taking Tabitha's shaking hand.

'She's all I've got.' Tears were threatening now, and Tabitha put her hand over her glass as the waiter returned, but Aiden had no such reserve. 'Just leave the bottle,' he ordered while waiting for Tabitha to continue. 'Gran brought me up after Mum and Dad died, devoted her life to me, and now she's old and lonely and terrified and there's nothing I can do. I've asked the bank for a loan, but the second you put ''dancer'' down as your occupation you might just as well rip up the application form.'

'Let me help you.' He ignored her furiously shaking head. 'Come on, darling, it would be a drop in the ocean. I haven't told you my good news yet. I sold a painting yesterday.'

'Aiden!' Despite her own problems, Tabitha's delighted squeal was genuine and, wrapping her arms around Aiden's neck, she planted a kiss on his cheek. 'That's fantastic news.'

'Please let me help you, Tabitha. You can always pay me back. We're on our way, darling.' Aiden grinned. 'I can feel it.'

But Tabitha shook her head. 'You might be, Aiden, but in my case "on my way out" would be a more apt description.' Her gloom descended again, but she did her best to keep the bitter note from her voice. 'I've been asked to audition for the next production.'

'So?' Aiden shrugged. 'You'll walk it.'

'Maybe, but it's always been automatic until now— I've always had a part. It's because I'm getting older.'

'You're twenty-four years old, for heaven's sake.'

'I'm twenty-nine,' Tabitha corrected, grinning despite herself. 'And twenty-nine-year-old dancers have a lot to prove. I can't borrow money from you when I've no idea if I'll be able to pay it back.'

'Please,' Aiden insisted, but Tabitha was adamant.

'No; I mean it, Aiden. I'm going to have to work this one out for myself.'

'You're sure?'

She nodded resolutely, and after a brief shrug Aiden let it go. 'I know it's abhorrent, seeing all this wealth when your grandmother's so broke, but money can be a curse, sometimes. The people here are so busy looking over their shoulders, sure everyone's after their last dollar, they honestly don't know who their real friends are. For all the highbrow people here you could count the true friends on one hand. If the money disappeared tomorrow so would ninety per cent of the guests, and that's probably a conservative estimate.'

'Your brother seems to have the impression that I'd be amongst them.'

Aiden's eyes narrowed. 'Tab, I'm sorry if he's been

giving you a hard time, but, though I'm loath to defend him for treating you appallingly, out of everyone here Zavier's got the most reason to be suspicious of people's motives, especially where women are concerned. He was let down pretty badly recently.'

'She must have been mad,' Tabitha mused.

'Stay clear, Tab. I mean it. A wonderful warm thing like you wouldn't last five minutes in his company. I might adore Zavier, but I wouldn't wish that black heart on my worst enemy. It could only end in tears. Anyway, you're here with me, remember? Don't you dare go blowing my cover by making smouldering eyes at my brother.'

Tabitha laughed. 'I wouldn't worry, Aiden. He's already made it abundantly clear what he thinks of me, and I can assure you it wasn't complimentary.' She grinned as Aiden winced. 'Any hot looks passing between us would probably be better described as fuming rather than smouldering. He's convinced I'm after you for your riches.'

'God.' Aiden added a couple more inches to his glass. 'Zavier couldn't be further from the mark if he tried; he'd have a fit if he knew the truth.'

Tabitha filled her own glass from the bottle, but unlike Aiden accepted a hefty splash of soda from a passing waiter. 'He has no idea, then?'

Aiden shrugged. 'I'm not sure. He tried to talk to me once—a big brother pep-talk would best describe it. You know the type: sort yourself out, grow up, what the hell's your problem?' He drained his glass in one gulp. 'He actually came right out and asked if I was gay.'

'So why didn't you tell him then? Would he have given you a hard time?'

Aiden shook his head. 'Zavier wouldn't care about something like that. Despite the fact he practically wears a suit and tie to bed he's pretty laid-back about that sort of thing.'

'Then why not tell him?'

'I figured it wouldn't be fair on him. There's no way I could tell my father, he'd have a coronary, and it would just be one more thing for Zavier to worry about. He carries the lot of us, you know.'

Tabitha was intrigued and leant closer. 'In what way?'

'Zavier runs the business. Dad's too sick now. I know he doesn't look it, but he's a walking time bomb—he needs heart surgery, but he's too much of a risk for an anaesthetic. No surgeon would touch him, particularly with the name Chambers.'

'But surely he can afford the best treatment?'

Aiden gave a low laugh. 'And the best lawyers. I'm no cardiac surgeon, but I can see where they're coming from. He's just too high-risk to even attempt surgery. And with his heart so weak that's even more of a reason not to tell him about me. It's better Zavier doesn't know—better that no one does.'

'Well, he doesn't,' Tabitha said soothingly. 'So you've got nothing to worry about.'

Still, as she took a sip, her eyes smarting as the liquor warmed its way down, she found her eyes instinctively combing the room, as if constantly drawn to the dark and foreboding man that utterly enthralled her.

He'd only break your heart, she consoled herself. But what a delicious way to go!

The party was getting louder now. People were dancing—kicking up their heels. Aiden swirled Tabitha around the dance floor a couple of times, but his heart clearly wasn't in it and he was only too happy to get back to the table and his never-ending supply of alcohol.

Tabitha was starting to wonder when they could reasonably make an exit to their hotel room upstairs. Her feet were killing her in the impossibly high sandals, and she thought her face might crack soon with the effort of smiling. There were also a couple of videos on the movie channel she wouldn't mind watching while Aiden slept off his excesses. She had more than returned Aiden's favour, and tomorrow she would tell him this had been the first and last time she would play the part of his girlfriend. Zavier's snide comments had seriously hit a nerve; the whole thing was starting to get out of hand. She would join the family for breakfast, make all the right noises, and then that would be it. Aiden would have to find someone else to fool his family.

Her hopes for a discreet exit were foiled, though, when Marjory descended with a grim-faced Zavier.

'There you are, darlings. How come you're not dancing?'

Tabitha forced a bright smile. 'Aiden's feeling a bit tired.'

'Well, that's no reason for *you* not to be dancing.' For an awful moment Tabitha thought Marjory was suggesting they grab their handbags and dance around them together! The reality was far worse. 'Zavier, why don't you take Tabitha for a dance?'

She braced herself for rejection. Zavier Chambers didn't look like the kind of man who did anything he didn't want to, and after the way he had addressed her earlier she was dismally confident of one thing: dancing with a money-grabbing gold-digger wouldn't be high on his list of priorities. Not that she wanted to dance; ten minutes alone with this man had truly terrified her.

'I'd love to.'

She looked up with a start, and as he offered his hand had no choice but to accept. Standing, she turned somewhat anxiously over to Aiden for some support, but he really was the worse for wear now.

Zavier's hand was hot and dry, closing over hers tightly. As he led her to the dance floor Tabitha had the strangest urge to make a bolt for it, to wrench her hand away and run to the safety of her hotel room. As if sensing her trepidation, he closed his hand more tightly on hers, only letting go when they were in the middle of the tightly packed dance floor.

Slipping his hand around her slender waist, he rested it there. She could feel the heat through her flimsy dress. A couple dancing past bumped her, forcing her closer to him. Zavier gripped her more tightly, steadying her as she toppled slightly.

'You're having a terrible night, aren't you?' He had to stoop to meet her ear, and as he did he held her closer. His hot breath tickled her earlobes, and despite the heat of the room Tabitha broke out in goosebumps as she felt his hands tighten around the small of her back.

'Of course I'm not. Everyone's been charming,' she lied, in what she hoped was a convincing voice.

But Zavier begged to differ. 'You've been sitting on your own most of the night, trying to pretend you don't mind. I've been watching you.'

That he'd noticed Tabitha found strangely touching; that he'd been watching her she found pleasantly disturbing. But she didn't answer at first. His hands on her back were having the strangest effect. All she wanted to do was rest her head on his chest, to let the heavy beat of the music fill her, to lose herself in the moment.

'So this is a sympathy dance?'

'No, I don't do anything out of sympathy.'

She wanted so badly to believe him, wanted to believe it was her stunning good looks that had brought him over—hell, she'd even settle for her witty personality—but the facts spoke for themselves: Marjory had commandeered the whole thing. 'I'm sorry.' Her voice was high and slightly breathless.

'For what?'

Dragging her eyes up, she was stunned to see the change in him; the icy stare had melted, replaced by the moist sheen of lust, but his dilated pupils in no way softened the intensity of his gaze. Running a tongue over her lips, she forced a reply, confused at the sudden shift in his demeanour. 'For you being forced to dance with me.'

He didn't say anything at first; then he bent his head and she felt the brush of his face against her hair. All her senses seemed to be standing rigid to attention.

'Don't be sorry,' he said huskily. 'After all, it's only a dance.'

This was the man who thought she was a conniving gold-digger—the man who had blatantly told her he was suspicious of her motives. But he was also the man holding her now, making her feel more of a woman than she had ever felt in her life. Everything about him forced her senses into overdrive: the exotic heady scent of him, the expensive cut of his suit beneath her fingers, the quiet strength of the arms holding her, the scratch of his cheek against hers. She gave up fighting it then. Nestling against his chest, she swayed slowly against him, relaxed under his skilful touch. Closing her eyes she inhaled deeply, every sense in her body attuned to the perfection of the moment.

It wasn't only a dance.

To describe it as such was a travesty.

CHAPTER THREE

'LET'S get you upstairs.' Aiden was slumped over the table but still managing to cling on to his half-empty glass. Shaking him on the shoulder, Tabitha whispered loudly in his ear. 'Come on, Aiden. People are starting to look—you really ought to be in bed.'

'Having trouble?' She could hear the derisive tone in Zavier's voice as he took in the situation.

'We're fine,' Tabitha said through gritted teeth, unable to meet his eyes after the dance they had shared, confused at the response he had so easily evoked in her and determined not to let him see.

'You don't look it,' he said knowingly.

'Well, we are. Aiden and I are just about to head off upstairs to bed.'

'Have you already called for a forklift or did you want me to ring for you?' His biting sarcasm only inflamed her taut nerves.

'He's just tired.' Tabitha said defensively, but she knew she wasn't fooling anyone—least of all Zavier.

'Ah, that's right; he's had a busy week at the studio. And there I was assuming that, as per usual, Aiden's the worse for wear. God, I'm such a cynic sometimes.'

People were really staring now; she could see Jeremy Chambers starting to make his way across the room, a questioning look on his face. A drunken showdown with his father was the last thing Aiden needed—her too, come to that.

Swallowing her pride, Tabitha bit back a smart reply.

Jeremy was nearly upon them now, and she had no choice but to accept Zavier's help if she wanted to avoid a scene.

'I could use a hand,' she admitted reluctantly.

'A "please" would be nice.'

She wasn't that desperate! 'Look, are you going to help or not?'

He smiled then—a real smile, that for a fleeting moment lit up his face. 'Okay, come on, let's get him upstairs.'

Which was easier said than done. They managed to get him out of the function room in a reasonably dignified fashion, but once they got to the lift Aiden slumped on his brother and proceeded to snore loudly.

Tabitha willed the lift to move faster; Zavier's close proximity in this confined space was not having the most calming effect on her. Still, it was just as well Zavier was there, Tabitha conceded, or she'd never have managed otherwise.

Aiden steadfastly refused to wake up, let alone walk, and in the end Zavier had to resort to giving him a fireman's lift—something he managed amazingly well, considering Aiden stood well over six feet. Tabitha retrieved the swipe card from Aiden's top pocket, holding the door open as Zavier made his way in and deposited his younger brother unceremoniously on the bed.

'Be sure to tell him how badly he behaved in the morning.'

'Oh, I'll tell him all right,' Tabitha said, her annoyance with Aiden apparent in her voice. 'And thanks for all your help getting him upstairs,' she added grudgingly.

'Don't mention it. I'm just glad he had the foresight to book a room here or we'd be stuck in the back of a taxi now. As you probably gathered, it's not the first time

I've had to come to my hapless brother's rescue. I'm sure it won't be the last.' He stared at her then, openly stared, until Tabitha was blushing to the tips of her painted toenails. 'I would have thought he'd have toned things down a bit by now, though—the love of a good woman and all that.'

'But I'm not good...' The words slipped seductively from her mouth before she could stop them, and she saw the start in his eyes at her provocative statement. Stunned, confused at her own behaviour, Tabitha attempted to retrieve herself. 'I mean from what you said to me at the reception...'

'Oh, I'm sure you have your good points.'

Despite the fact they were occupying one of the Windsor's most opulent suites, suddenly the room seemed incredibly small. There was something big going on here—more than just a gentle flirting. Everything about Zavier screamed danger. Every nerve in her tense body seemed to be on high alert, the fight or flight response triggered by his proximity overwhelming her, but there was nowhere to run and, even more disturbing, Tabitha wasn't sure that she wanted to.

She wanted badly to dazzle him with some witty response, to show she was completely in control, not remotely fazed by his imposing presence, but she wasn't in control here—far from it. Zavier Chambers seemed to trigger a major physiological reaction in her just being in the same room.

Void of any reply, Tabitha busied herself removing Aiden's shoes. Pulling a thick blanket from the wardrobe, she covered his limp body.

She was confident Zavier would go now, which would enable her to at least catch her breath again. After all, he had delivered Aiden safely—had done his brotherly duty. There was no reason for him to stay now—no logical one anyway.

'I ought to put him on his side, in case he's sick,' Tabitha said, more to herself than in an attempt at small talk. Pushing her arms under Aiden, she knelt on the bed, pulling his back towards her.

'Careful—you might hurt yourself.' In an instant Zavier leant over to help her, his hand catching her arm as he attempted to render assistance. But the contact was too much for Tabitha's already shot nerves and she pulled her arm back swiftly.

His coolness only exacerbated her nervousness. She felt his eyes flicker over her exposed cleavage, and as if in response her nipples stiffened, protruding against the flimsy fabric. Even as she swallowed nervously she felt as if he was registering the tiny movement in her throat.

'Tabitha…' Aiden, slurring his words, struggled to sit up. 'Sorry.'

'Don't worry about it now,' Tabitha said gently. 'Just try and sleep.'

Aiden's squinting eyes locked on her. 'I mean it, Tab, I'm really sorry. I've been thinking,' he slurred, resting back on the pillow, 'I should just marry you. You know that? It would solve everything.'

She felt more than saw Zavier stiffen, heard the tiniest hiss come from his lips, and knew that Zavier thought this was a proposal she had somehow engineered. Her own shock at Aiden's suggestion for a moment put on hold, she attempted to quiet her friend. But it was too late. The words had escaped, seeping through the air like a vile vapour, compounding every last one of Zavier's suspicions.

'Don't be silly.' Tabitha attempted a light scold, a

nervous giggle escaping her lips. 'Why would you say such a thing?'

All Aiden could manage was a small shrug before closing his eyes again, but Zavier wanted answers. Reaching over, he shook his brother, rattling him none too gently.

'Come on, Aiden,' he quipped, his light voice belying the muscle pounding in his cheek. 'That's no way to propose to a lady.' She saw the tiny snarl as his lips formed around the words. 'Finish what you've started.'

'It would solve everything,' Aiden mumbled. 'Dad would see a marriage before he dies—' he squinted at Tabitha, who stood mortified '—and your gambling debts would be taken care of, darling. I know how worried you...' He never finished his sentence, instead choosing that moment to go into a deep and rather noisy sleep.

'I can explain...' Tabitha started. 'It's not how it seems.'

Zavier flashed her a thin smile. 'I'm sure it's far worse.'

'It isn't. The gambling debts—'

He halted her with one flick of his manicured hand, his gold watch glinting in the bedside light. 'I don't give a damn what trouble you're in. You, Miss Reece, don't concern me—not one iota. But understand this.' His voice was menacing. 'Stay away from my brother. Marry him and I'll expose you for what you are—a cheap, conniving gold-digger. Do I make myself clear?'

'You don't understand.'

'Oh, yes, I do,' he hissed. Coming around the bed, he stood over her, stepping uninvited into her personal space, so close she could feel the scorn of his words on her cheek—so close, so vividly near, even the batting of his eyelids seemed to be happening in slow motion. 'You think you've got it all worked out, don't you? You think the Chambers family are going to be the answer to whatever mess you've got yourself into.'

'I don't.' She was trying to defend herself, trying to form an argument, but his presence, his closeness, wasn't just intimidating her now; it was overwhelming her, fogging her mind with dangerous images. The scent she had inhaled on the dance floor was stifling her now, conjuring recollections of their one dance, and her subconscious responded as it had when he held her. 'I don't,' she said again, dragging her eyes up to meet his, trying to sound as if she meant it, trying to ignore the surge of adrenaline cascading through her body—the high alert of imminent impact.

His Adam's apple moved as he swallowed. Already he was wearing the dusky growth of a five o'clock shadow, and she imagined the scratch of his cheek on hers, the roughness behind his kiss. Though she hated the venom of his attack, Tabitha was curiously excited, high on adrenaline and champagne and the heady cocktail of hormones his presence haplessly triggered.

His hand moved up slowly and she stood frozen. Only the none too gentle sound of Aiden's snoring broke the silence—only that and the pounding in her temples as he traced a finger along her white collarbone, exploring the hollows of her neck, his fingers brushing under her curls.

And she waited.

Waited for him to jerk her towards him, to expel the tension with the roughest of kisses. She licked her lips, her pink tongue bobbing out involuntarily, moistening her flesh in anticipation.

'I might have known.' In one harsh movement, one

harsh sentence, reality invaded and his fingers flipped out the designer label on her dress. 'Is that the going price for a date these days?'

His words confused her. Struggling to understand his meaning, she stepped back, the distance giving her a chance to collect her thoughts as the contempt in his eyes flared.

'I sign off Aiden's credit cards,' he explained nastily. 'I should have worked it out earlier. Your outfit is the only tasteful thing about you.'

'Get out.'

'Oh, I'm going, and in the morning, Tabitha, so are you. As far from my family as humanely possible if you know what's good for you.'

Only when the door was safely closed, when only the heavy masculine scent of him remained, did Tabitha breathe again.

Not trusting her legs to stand, she sat on the edge of the sofa, practically trembling just at the thought of him. He was vile, loathsome, full of his own self-importance—and yet... Never had a man made such an impact on her. Those few moments on the dance floor with him had tapped rivers of passion she hadn't even realised existed. His eyes had seemed to tear through her, his mouth, his smell...

And there wasn't a single thing she could do about it! Even if she could stretch the boundaries of truth and imagine someone as completely stunning as Zavier Chambers ever in a million years being attracted to her, she was supposed to be his brother's gold-digging girl-friend—with a gambling problem to boot! Completely out of bounds by anyone's standards.

Stretching out on the long sofa, she lay staring at the ceiling, almost weeping with frustration at the unfairness of it all. Even the movie channel held no attraction now. What was the point? The real thing had been in this very room only moments before!

It was only a few seconds later when she realised she'd left her bag down at the party.

Rolling on to her side, she battled with the urge to go and retrieve it—battled with the urge to return to the party and a chance of glimpsing Zavier again. It would look stupid, she reasoned. He would surely realise the motive behind it. But her reasoning, however logical, however sensible, was no match for her desire—her need to somehow finish whatever dangerous game had been started, to put him right, to draw a conclusion or open Pandora's box.

She simply couldn't just leave it there.

Opening the door, Tabitha made her way along the thickly carpeted corridor, her heart beating loudly, her pulse rapid and out of time with the music pounding below.

The dark, shadowy figure making its way towards her was so broad, so tall, it could only belong to one person.

A couple more steps and his face came into focus, his eyes glittering and dark, a curious look of triumph on his face.

'Looking for this?' He held up her bag, the splash of feminine colour an enticing contrast against such a masculine backdrop. 'I was back down at the party and I saw it lying under the table.'

'Thank you.' She accepted the bag but didn't turn back, unable to tear her eyes away from his penetrating gaze.

'Fancy a nightcap?'

Even as Tabitha nodded her acceptance she knew he didn't intend to take her back down to the bar, and for that moment at least she wouldn't have had it any other way.

His room was amazingly tidy. A few heavy bottles and brushes adorned the dresser, and a half-drunk glass of whisky was on the coffee table. Tabitha noticed the ice-cubes undissolved; he hadn't gone straight back down to the wedding after he'd left her.

His eyes followed hers to the glass; his steady voice answered the unasked question.

'I was trying to figure out a legitimate excuse to see you again tonight. Contrary to the lecture I'll be delivering to Aiden in the morning, sometimes the answer does come in a bottle.' He looked at her bemused expression. 'I was sitting here thinking about you, wondering if I could risk ringing you, then it dawned on me you didn't have your bag...'

'Why did you need an excuse? I mean, why did you want to see me again? Haven't you quite finished lecturing me?'

'Lectures over.'

Could this be happening to her? Had Zavier Chambers sat nursing his whisky filled with the same trembling desire that had overcome her as she lay on the sofa? Surely it wasn't possible? 'So why did you come looking for me?'

'Isn't that obvious?'

She had stared at the glass long enough. Dragging her eyes up to his, she was shocked and strangely excited to see the same blatant desire emanating from them that had turned her to liquid on the dance floor. 'I thought you hated me.'

He shook his head slowly, deliberately. 'It's a rather more basic feeling you evoke in me at the moment.'

How could this be happening to her? How could

someone as charismatic and overtly sexual as Zavier possibly be interested in her, possibly want her? He could have any woman he wanted. He held her gaze, pinning her with his eyes. Everything about tonight seemed surreal, as if she were caught up in some strange erotic dream.

'Come here.' His voice was low, his request direct.

Tabitha knew that she should have left right there and then—picked up her bag, thanked him for his help and got the hell out of there.

But she didn't.

Tentatively she stepped towards him, drawn by an overwhelming longing that transcended all else.

She was completely out of her depth, overcome with desire. Never in her wildest dreams could she have imagined acting so boldly, yet Zavier imbued in her a feeling of wantonness—desires so basic, feelings so overwhelming that for now she couldn't even begin to deal with the consequences, couldn't contemplate anything other than what was happening right here and now. One look into his dark brooding eyes and a whole lifetime of scruples needed rewriting.

'Dance.'

Mesmerised, she nodded, her hand reaching out for him, desperate to feel him again, to revisit the magic they had created on the dance floor. But Zavier had other ideas. Almost imperceptibly he shook his head.

'No. Dance *for* me.'

His eyes left hers for the briefest impatient moment, his fingers working a remote control and the room filling with the low sensual throb of bass, the straining tears of a violin. And though it moved her, though the music fuelled her, it didn't even come close to the rush of desire that flooded her as his gaze returned.

'I can't.' Her tongue flicked over dry lips. 'I can't,' she said again when he didn't answer. 'You'll laugh at me.'

Again he shook his head. 'I'm not laughing, Tabitha; I want to see you dance. Dance for me like you do when you're alone.'

He knew! Like a child caught singing into a hairbrush, she felt the sting of embarrassment. It was as if he had an open ticket to her mind, her dreams—as if he had seen her pushing back the coffee table at home, pulling the curtains and dancing as she would have if only her ambitions had been fulfilled.

It was the most ridiculous of requests, one that under absolutely any other circumstance would have been laughable. But there was no mirth in his voice, not even a note of challenge, just the thick throb of lust and a million fantasies that needed to be fulfilled, imbuing her with the confidence of a woman who could fulfil them, the empowering realisation that though it was Zavier calling the shots it was she, Tabitha, fulfilling them.

The straps on her sandals were fiddly, her hair falling forward as her shaking hands worked the tiny buckles. She was incredulous that she was even contemplating obliging him, but as the music filled the room it overtook her awkwardness, the throbbing sensual rhythm fuelling her. Slowly she slid her toes up the long length of her calf, the wraparound dress falling apart to reveal taut flexed muscles. Instinctively tightening her stomach, she felt the imaginary string that pulled dancers taller snap taut. She let the music take over, washing over her body as, like liquid silk, she moved to the beat, swaying, turning, dancing the most private of dances for the most captive of audiences. And when the music slowed, when, breathless, her body glimmering, she dared to look at him, the blaze of desire emanating from his expressive eyes took the last of her breath away.

'Come here.'

It was the second time he had beckoned her, the second time he had summoned her, and Tabitha knew the interlude was over—knew this time when she went to him exactly how the scene would end.

Tabitha had never been promiscuous; to date her relationships had always been taken seriously. She wasn't a woman who could be bought with meals and flowers, her heart wasn't something to be given away lightly, but as she crossed the room, as she took that tentative step off the cliff-edge and into areas unknown, her mind was whirring, her love-life passing before her eyes in those fateful final moments before passion completely took over.

With blinding realisation she knew why she was doing this—or, more importantly, why she wanted to do this. Meals, flowers—they all made her feel wanted, feminine, sexy. Zavier Chambers had done in a few hours what most men took months to achieve. He had made her feel completely a woman.

He stood absolutely still as she crossed the room, drawing her towards him with an animal magnetism, but as she drew nearer his arms shot up, pulling her close, dragging her from her cliff-edge as if one split second was too long to be apart.

The weight of his lips on hers was explosive, hungry. She almost cried out at the impact of him against her, her lips parting as he probed her with his tongue. She could taste the lingering traces of whisky, the sharp scent of his maleness filling her senses.

His hair was thick and silken under her fingers, his thighs hard and solid as he pulled her nearer, and she could feel his arousal, urgent and solid. Pulling at her hairclips, he threw them almost angrily to the floor, his fingers spilling her Titian curls, coaxing them around her face. Pushing her head back, he let his lips explore her neck, scratching the soft skin with his chin as his sensual mouth located the flickering pulse there.

He pulled away. 'Are you sure?'

His voice was thick, rasping, and the question was thoughtful. But she was beyond any rationale. The whys and wherefores would have to wait; for now only the moment mattered. She stood quivering, only his arms holding her up. The only thing she was sure about was that if he stopped kissing her now, stopped ravishing her, adoring her with his body, she would die with frustration. Her voice came out gasping, unsteady. 'Please,' she urged, 'don't stop.'

For the first time since their lips had met she opened her eyes. He was staring down at her, his pupils dilated, desire burning in every facet of his being.

'Don't stop,' she urged again.

It was all the affirmation he needed to continue and, swooping her into his embrace, Zavier carried her towards the bedroom. Ripping back the smooth counterpane, he laid her on the huge bed.

What Tabitha had expected she had no idea—for him to tear at her clothes, for her to rip at his shirt? But the animal passion that had gripped them in the lounge suite dimmed a notch, replaced instead by a sensual hum, an almost reverent admiration as he slowly pulled down her zipper, savouring each first glimpse of her exposed flesh.

Planting slow, deep kisses on her shoulders, he pulled down her straps, exploring her clavicle with his tongue. She heard his sharp intake of breath as the chiffon slipped over her breasts. Her pink nipples begged for the coolness of his tongue, flicking each taut nipple until it was swollen and aching, dancing to his probing attendance. Down ever down, he moved, across the white hollow of her stomach to the glistening silken Titian curls hiding her amber treasure box, which he opened with wonder, his tongue working its magic again, making her gasp as he brought her ever nearer to the brink of oblivion. Then, abating slightly, leaving her hovering on the brink, on the edge of the universe, he worked slowly on the delicately freckled expanse of flesh that spilled out over her sheer stockings.

With cat-like grace he stood up, his eyes never leaving hers as he undid his shirt, and though the music had stopped long ago his hips gyrated slowly to a beat of their own. Only his eyes were still, watching her reaction at the first glimpse of the ebony mat of hair on his chest, inking down over his flat stomach. She heard his zipper slide down, followed the plane of ebony as his trousers slid down his solid thighs, revealing the first heady glimpse of his manhood, trapped and writhing in his underwear. She reached towards him, her trembling hand aching, desperate to touch him, but Zavier shook his head, taunting her a while longer as he slowly took off the last remnants of clothing.

It was the most sensual thing she had ever witnessed, a teasing ritual that whetted her appetite. What she had expected from his lovemaking she hadn't dared even imagine. A cool aloofness, perhaps, a distance despite their closeness? Not this teasing disrobing for her benefit, this naked display of sensuality, this sheer, delicious decadence. He pushed her gently back onto the bed, the rough hair on his thighs scratching through the silk of her stockings as he parted her legs, diving into her with such precision and force that she cried out in abandonment, her legs coiling around his waist, whilst her coral-painted nails dug into his taut buttocks.

And finally the only dance left was the dance of lovers entwined, their bodies making music of their own, dancing to a private rhythm, a jazz of harmonic idioms in tune with each other, improvising as they went. The rhythm filled them, fuelled them, spurring them on, finding out what worked, what mixed—and it all did. Every last cell in their bodies seemed to be sated with desire until she could hold back no longer. Every pulse in her body had aligned, focusing towards her very epicentre as he exploded within her. Gasping, her body throbbing, she opened her eyes. She needed to see him at this moment—see the man who had brought her to this magical place. For he was the perfection she craved, he was the ultimate fantasy, and she was living it, loving it.

To close her eyes now would only taint the dream.

'What about Aiden?'

His question filtered through the haze, unwelcome and unexpected, the harshness in his voice such a stark contrast to the husky endearments of only moments before.

'Tabitha?'

She heard the impatient note, the summons for an explanation. Pulling up the heavy white sheet, she tucked it around her, her eyes darting to his, reeling with shock at the contempt so visible, stunned at the change in his demeanour.

Sitting up, she pulled the sheet closer, covering her breasts while knowing it was way too late for false modesty, bemused at the sudden change in him. 'I can explain...' she started, running a hand through the riot of curls, searching her mind for an answer. But she didn't have one. Telling the truth to Zavier might redeem her somewhat, but at what price? Betraying her dearest friend simply wasn't an option; Aiden's secret wasn't hers to share.

He turned his head then, just a fraction, enough for his eyes to burn into her shoulder, to see her stiffen as he carried on. 'If you love him then tell me, Tabitha, just what are you doing in bed with me? I mean, surely even you can see that this is stretching the boundaries of decency. I guess anyone can make a mistake in the heat of passion, but surely you would have put up a bit of a fight if you truly loved Aiden? I thought I'd at least have to try a bit harder to get you into my room.'

It took a moment to gather her thoughts, to take in all he was saying, but suddenly with vile realisation she saw what he had done. He might have been attracted to her, he might have wanted her, but going through with it— inviting her to his room, seducing her—had all been a test. A test to see if she truly loved his brother, if she could fight the attraction of another man.

And she had failed, dismally failed.

'You set me up?' Her lips were white, her voice shaking.

Zavier laughed. 'Possibly, though I didn't sense much resistance.'

'You set me up,' she repeated, angry now, shocked and hurt at what he had done. 'You were testing me, trying to see how far I'd go.' With a whimper of horror she recalled Aiden's words. *'He'd crush you in the palm of his hand.'*

Zavier Chambers had done just that. He was as inscrutable as he was dangerous, and she had only herself to blame for playing right into his hands.

Grabbing the sheet around her, Tabitha leapt out of bed. Retrieving her flimsy dress and underwear from the floor, she ran into the bathroom. Slamming the door, she grappled with the lock—but he was too quick for her. Forcing the bathroom door open, he strode in. His nudity embarrassed her now, hurt her, a shocking reminder of what she had done. Averting her eyes, she pulled tighter at the sheet. Her eyes sparkled with tears and she squeezed them shut.

Mercifully, he reacted to her embarrassment and tucked a towel around himself before firmly taking hold of her arm and turning her to face him.

'Stay away from Aiden,' he hissed, his face menacingly close.

'Get your hands off me.' Her voice was amazingly calm—authoritative, even; her shock had been replaced now with a burning anger. 'You don't know all the facts. The truth of the matter is that I'm actually doing your damn family a favour by being here.'

'By making sure we don't find out Aiden's gay?' His sneering reply simultaneously shocked and confused her.

'You already know?'

'Of course I know, and if I hadn't been sure tonight only confirmed it!'

'Why?' Her mind was reeling, shocked by the revelation, wondering what Aiden's reaction would be.

He let her go then, but Tabitha didn't move. Her eyes searched his face, demanding an answer, and when it came it was barely audible, his voice a throaty low whisper that she had to strain to catch. 'Any other man would have been proud to have you on his arm.'

Tabitha let out a nervous giggle that was completely out of place given the animosity between them. 'I'm hardly Amy Dellier.'

'You're ten of Amy Dellier,' Zavier spat. 'And if Aiden had an ounce of testosterone in him just what the hell was he doing holding his whisky glass instead of you?'

'If you know he's gay then I don't see why you're so angry. Surely you know I can't be after him for his money...'

'Oh, spare me the speeches,' Zavier spat. 'Do you really think yours would be the first marriage of convenience? And I'm not talking about the general population either. The whole Chambers family tree is littered with rotten apples—sweet little things on the outside, rotten greedy gold-diggers on the inside.'

'I don't know what you're talking about!' Her voice was rising now, her shame at having slept with him wrestling with her anger at the way she was being treated and, worst of all, her cringing embarrassment at how easily she had let him in, at the side of her she had so readily exposed.

'Take this wedding, my cousin Simone...' He threw his hands up in the air in a wildly exaggerated gesture. 'Love's young dream, my foot.' He looked at her bemused face. 'You want an example closer to home? My parents, then.'

'But—but they seem so happy,' Tabitha stammered.

'Happy, yes. Married, yes. But happily married is another thing entirely. And if you think I'm going to let you get your claws into Aiden you can think again.'

'He was joking,' Tabitha pleaded, but it fell on deaf ears.

'No, he wasn't, Tabitha,' Zavier said darkly. 'For all his arty ways, for all the alternative lifestyle you and Aiden insist on living, you're both as shallow as it comes. You can buck the system all you want but you still like your bills paid, you still like your little luxuries—and what a luxurious life it would be,' he sneered.

'How respectable Mrs Tabitha Chambers would be once her gambling debts were paid off. I can see you now at bridge parties, or at the Melbourne Cup. Far less sordid than the places you probably frequent now. The only problem with that little scenario is you're a hot little thing.' He moved closer now, his breath warm on her already scorching cheeks. 'The gambling tables aren't the only place you get your kicks, are they?'

'You don't know what you're saying.' Her voice was strangled, a strained whisper, yet she couldn't move, standing frozen like a rabbit trapped in headlights.

'Oh, yes, I do. You'd have to take a lover—discreetly, of course. Was that what this was about? Some sort of audition to see if I have the staying power to sustain you through a lonely loveless marriage?'

'Of course not.'

He dismissed her response with a toss of his head. 'I assume I passed.'

'You *assume* one hell of a lot,' Tabitha flared. 'You know what? I actually feel sorry for you. You're so sure everyone's out for your money, so sure we're all as hard as you. Is it so hard to believe in happily-ever-after?'

'After what?'

For a second she thought he was being facetious.

'After what?' he demanded again.

Still she thought he was joking, but on closer inspection he looked genuinely perplexed. 'Happily ever after,' she repeated, but still there was no reaction to indicate he understood. 'Like in the fairytales. Didn't your mother read you bedtime stories?'

Zavier laughed, but there was no humour behind it. 'You've met my mother. Can you really imagine her tucking us in with some namby-pamby fairytale?'

It had never entered her head that she might feel sorry

for Zavier Chambers. After all, he had everything she didn't—money, power, parents. And yet… Looking over at his haughty face, his brooding eyes, Tabitha was assailed with a sudden tidal wave of sympathy. Sure, she had only had her parents for seven years, but she wouldn't trade her memories for a lifetime of Marjory and Jeremy—tucked up in bed with her mother reading aloud as she took her on journeys to castles and princes and happy endings. A world where the good guy always won.

'You've got it all wrong,' Tabitha said, but more gently this time.

'Oh, I don't think so.'

Picking up her dress, he flashed one more look at the designer label before throwing it towards her.

'Stay away from my family, Tabitha Reece. You make me sick.'

CHAPTER FOUR

DANCING had always been her escape. So much more than a job, so much more than a means to an end. The throbbing music, the darkened audience, the sensual smell of bodies dancing, writhing. Losing herself to the rhythm, living only for the moment, the world on hold till the heavy dusty curtain descended.

But tonight there was no escape.

There hadn't been for five days.

Five long days and five even longer nights. Days spent chasing banks, building societies, waiting for the call that would save her grandmother, the gnawing panic of debt snapping at her heels. But they paled in comparison to the agony of the nights. Lonely nights waiting for a call of a different kind, tossing and turning, watching the moon drift past her window, the Southern Cross twinkling in the inky sky a constant reminder of her insignificance.

There was no refuge.

Now, as she danced, every response in her body, every surge of emotion seemed paltry, a pale imitation of what she had felt under Zavier's masterful touch.

A one-night stand. It sounded cheap, sordid—sexual gratification for the sake of it. A primitive meeting of desires, then walking away without a backward glance.

But it hadn't been like that for Tabitha. She hadn't walked away without a glance. Her mind was constantly there, remembering the bliss of him. He had hurt her, embarrassed her, humiliated her, yet...

51

In his arms, wrapped around his body, when the velvet endearments had poured like silk from his lips, she had found the solace she hadn't realised she'd craved, felt the mastery of his touch, glimpsed the impossible fantasy of being loved by Zavier.

Loved.

The word echoed through her mind like a mocking taunt.

There was nothing transitory about it.

So tonight Tabitha danced, danced because she had to, because it was her job, her livelihood, and she danced well—but nothing like the way she had for Zavier. And this time when the curtain came down she didn't rush off stage with the other dancers, because tonight there was no rush to get home, no haste to get into her large lonely bed and dream her impossible dreams.

The high-spirited chatter, the buzz of euphoria that came with the end of each show seemed to be in another language as she listlessly pulled off her costume, her dusty tights discarded on the even dustier main dressing room floor as Tabitha rummaged in her bag for her wrap.

'There's a Mr Chambers here to see you.' Marcus the stagehand sounded as put out as ever, and Tabitha gave him an apologetic smile as she turned to greet her friend. Aiden was becoming a regular feature backstage, his excuses to Marcus legendary as he wrestled with a reason not to drink alone.

'So what was the crisis tonight? Has your pet goldfish finally succumbed…?'

Her teasing sentence died on her lips as she stared into the face of Zavier, as familiar as her own, the face that had filled her dreams, fuelled her imagination since the moment she met him.

'Nothing quite so dramatic.' He made his way over,

the sea of dancers parting, staring shamelessly from him to Tabitha, undisguised admiration on their faces. 'I have to go to America in the morning and I thought we ought to go over some details.'

'Details?' Her perplexed voice was barely audible as she stared at him dumbfounded.

Only as his eyes flicked down to her pink, glistening body did she become acutely aware of the fact that all she was wearing was a flesh-coloured G-string. It had never been an issue—the changing room was permanently littered with naked bodies—but under Zavier's gaze there was nothing casual in her nakedness, no innocence in the way her body responded to his mere presence. She had dreamed of this moment, determined that when—if—she ever saw him again, she would look cool and aloof; she had even gone so far as to practise in the mirror—a gentle furrowing of her brow, a slight snap of her fingers as she tried to recall his name.

A wasted effort.

There was nothing sophisticated in the way he had found her, nothing aloof about the burning blush creeping over her near-naked body.

'The wedding—it's only four weeks away. We really ought to be finalising a few things.' The usual post-performance gaggle was deathly quiet, every ear straining to hear, every eye on them. 'Marcus?'

She vaguely registered Zavier turn to the stagehand, noticing how strange it was that he knew his name, how even Marcus seemed only too happy to please the might that was Zavier Chambers.

'Is there somewhere we could go? Somewhere a bit more private?' He flashed a malevolent smile at a mute Tabitha. 'My fiancée looks as if she might need to sit down.'

It only took a moment to dress, to drape her wrap around her, to pull on her short Lycra skirt and slip on some sandals, but it felt like a lifetime. The eyes of her colleagues, her friends, her boss, were on her, but they didn't compare to the heavy stare of Zavier, the impatience in his stance as she fiddled to tie her wrap.

Of course when you are Zavier Chambers your affairs aren't expected to be discussed in a dusty backstage dressing room. Doors open, or rather *private* dressing room doors open. Five-star ones, with mirrors and mini bars. And, though it was a world she inhabited daily, such sumptuous surroundings were painfully unfamiliar. Zavier immediately made himself at home, tossing aside his jacket and pulling a bottle out of the fridge with all the arrogance of a man who was used to having the best of everything.

'What's all this about?' Her voice, which had failed her for the past few minutes, didn't sound as assured as Tabitha would have liked, but it would have to do. 'How dare you just barge in here? How dare you stroll in and drop a bombshell like that, only to leave me to pick up the pieces? I have to work with these people.'

'Chambers wives don't work,' came the swift riposte. Annoyingly unmoved by her anger, he popped a champagne cork with ease and filled two glasses. He handed her one, topping up the pale liquid until the bubbles flooded her trembling hands.

'I mean it, Zavier. I want you to tell me what all this is about!'

'It's really very simple.' He flashed that dangerous smile. 'It's about us.'

Us?

It was hard to remain focused on the words coming

from him as she lost herself in the simple word. Us. You and I. Him and I. Me and you. You and me.

The simplest of words with the biggest of connotations.

'What us?'

'Us getting married.'

He said it so lightly, so easily, that for a moment Tabitha didn't even register his words, her mind too much filled with remembering when his lips had been closer, the taste of his cool tongue exploring hers. It was only after a few seconds that she parted the fog where her brain had once been and his statement filtered through.

'Married?'

'That's right.' Zavier nodded.

'Marry you?'

'Right again.' The dressing room, not big, seemed to have taken on minuscule proportions. It wasn't just his size that was daunting; everything about him oozed confidence and over-abundance. She felt like Alice in Wonderland in reverse, as the walls seemed to close in around her. Actually—Tabitha shook her head ruefully—maybe she wasn't so far off with her fairytale analogy. A proposal from someone like Zavier Chambers was the stuff of pure fantasy. It must be every girl's dream that a man as infinitely desirable might say those three little words while looking into your eyes. Except there wasn't a hint of romance in the air, and from the way he was distractedly examining his fingernails, tapping his well-shod foot on the floorboards as he waited for Tabitha to speak, it was clear Zavier wasn't about to whisk her off to live happily ever after.

'Why on earth would you ask me to marry you?' The

anger had gone from her voice now, replaced instead by sheer bewilderment.

'Because for once one of Aiden's hare-brained schemes actually has some merit.'

'But all I agreed to was a date. The marriage proposal was as much a surprise to me as it was to you. Why won't you believe me when I say I'm not after your brother? I never have been. It was a simple matter of helping him out—not some contrived plan to rob him blind. And for your information I spoke about it with Aiden the following morning, when he repeated his offer, and again I said no.'

'I'm aware of that,' Zavier replied easily, examining his manicured nails closely, not even bothering to look up as he spoke. 'And I must admit somewhat surprised too. Were you holding out for more?'

Dumbly she shook her head.

'I can't say I blame you,' Zavier carried on, ignoring her denial. 'After all, Aiden's hardly a safe bet.' He shot her a dry smile. 'We all know how you like a gamble, but why stack the odds against you with a penniless artist who could be disinherited? Why expose yourself to the risk of his family finding out the truth behind your little sham and run the risk of ending up penniless?'

'You've got it all wrong.'

'I don't think so,' Zavier said with a thin smile that definitely didn't meet his eyes. 'Anyway, for once in your life, Tabitha, you win. This time, darling, you've hit the jackpot.'

'What jackpot?' Her lips were curled in the beginning of a sneer, her nerves at seeing him momentarily overridden by the preposterousness of his words.

'I'm raising the stakes.' His eyes narrowed and he left his nails, examining her closely now, watching her colour mount under his scrutiny. 'That's the bit you like, isn't it?' he hissed.

But Tabitha refused to be bullied. Yes, he was intimidating, and, yes, he was undoubtedly the most powerful man she had ever come up against. Yet she had seen another side to him, been held by him, ravished by him, adored by him albeit fleetingly.

Fear didn't come into it.

'If I was confused before, you've completely lost me now,' Tabitha admitted with a slightly exaggerated sigh, then gratefully took a sip of champagne, because it was the only thing she could do other than look into his eyes.

'For once in his gormless life Aiden actually had an idea that might have some merit.'

He watched as she sat down at the dressing table, watched as she took some tissues and wiped the livid red lipstick from her lips, pulled out the jangle of pins that held her Titian locks.

He remembered with total recall the feel of those silken curls beneath his fingers, releasing the tight pins, running his hand to free them, the cool tumble of her hair as it cascaded down her pale shoulders, and realised he was clenching his fists, having to physically restrain himself from crossing the room and helping her.

'Maybe this will make things clearer.' His voice came out too harsh, too sharp, the quilted muscles in his face refusing nonchalance as he reached into his suit and laid a cheque in front of her.

'This is a joke, right?'

'I've never been more serious in my life.'

Her hands were working faster now, pulling out the pins with impatience, and apart from a brief cursory glance downwards, to see what he was doing, her eyes never left the mirror. She had no desire to examine it more closely—no desire to see the undoubtedly ludicrous figure he was offering for her services.

'I suggest you take a closer look,' he said, his voice deep, his eyes boring into her shoulder. 'It's not every day one gets offered this amount of money.'

'It's not every day one gets to be made to feel a tart.'

Her words were like a slap to his cheek and Zavier involuntarily winced. 'That isn't my intention.' His response sounded genuine, almost apologetic, but, clearing his throat, he carried on in a more impassive voice. 'It's merely a solution to a problem.'

'What *problem*?'

'You have major financial problems; I have a father who longs to see one of his children married. Time isn't on my side, and from what Aiden's told me you're up against the clock to come up with some money. You're up to your neck in debt.'

'No.' The violence behind her denial literally brought Tabitha to her feet. 'I'm not.'

He didn't move a muscle, didn't even deign to look at her. 'Why do you need money, then?'

It did enter her mind to tell him—she even opened her lips to speak. But it dawned on her then that telling Zavier the truth would end things here and now. If Zavier knew the debt was her grandmother's rather than hers then their conversation would effectively be over. And, though his suggestion of marriage was as preposterous as it was ludicrous, Tabitha was intrigued and, perhaps more pointedly, ten minutes more of Zavier's time were ten minutes she craved.

'I don't want to talk about it.'

'I bet you don't,' he snapped, before taking a deep, steadying breath. 'I'm offering you a way out, a solution to our respective problems.' He pushed the cheque towards her again, and this time Tabitha did look, her eyes flicking down to the extravagant scrawl, widening as they saw they impossibly huge figure. 'This is part-payment.'

'Part-payment?'

'On acceptance,' he said, his tone businesslike. 'You'll get the same amount again after the wedding, and double that in six months—providing, of course, you've been a good wife.'

'A good wife?' The bewilderment in her voice was audible even to Tabitha, and she mentally kicked herself for repeating his words. She sounded like a parrot.

'No scandal, no talking to the press, and no objections to a quick divorce.'

'D-divorce?' A parrot with a stammer, Tabitha thought ruefully, focusing on anything other than the ridiculous conversation that was taking place.

He gave a wry smile. 'I'm not expecting you to sign your life away—just six months.' He gave a small shrug, but Tabitha knew the nonchalant gesture hid a lot of pain. 'My father's been given three months to live at best. Six months will give a respectable time-frame before the family hits the headlines again. Otherwise, it might look a touch callous for you to leave me so soon after his death. I'm not out to trash your reputation.'

'Just to trash my self-respect.'

'I think you've already taken care of that,' he said nastily, and Tabitha felt her colour rise as she remembered just how quickly she had jumped into bed with him. But as he continued she realised he wasn't alluding to their one night together—her vice, as he saw it, wasn't for impossibly handsome dark-haired men with enough sex appeal to set the world on fire. 'There'll also be no more gambling. Naturally, given your weakness and the nature of our marriage, you'll understand that I shan't be making you a joint signatory on anything, but of course you'll have a substantial allowance. Aiden informs me that your debts were incurred in a casino, so I just ask that you stay away from gaming tables unless I'm present—at least while we're married. What you do after that is your business. You can put the whole lot on black, for all I care, when the divorce comes through, but it might be wise to use this time to get some help. I'm happy to pay for a counsellor.'

'That really won't be necessary.'

'Fine.' Zavier sighed. 'Addicts are always the last to see they have a problem. But if you change your mind the offer's there. Anyway, it's all outlined in the contract.'

Tabitha was about to repeat his last word, but managed to bite her lip as he produced two documents from his briefcase.

'I suggest you sit down to read it. It will take some time. I want you to be absolutely sure you know what you're getting into before you sign.'

He was talking as if she had agreed, as if the result was a foregone conclusion, and Tabitha's bemusement turned to anger. 'You really think I'm going to say yes to this ludicrous proposition?'

'Of course you are,' Zavier replied assuredly. 'This amount of money will change your life.'

'I'm quite happy with my life, thank you very much.'

'How long do you think you can carry on like this, Tabitha?'

She braced herself for a short, sharp lecture on the pitfalls of gambling, smugly confident that Zavier didn't have a clue what he was talking about, but when he spoke, the words that came from his lips literally floored her, chilled her. Every raw, shredded nerve, every silent fear, every sleepless night, were all summed up in one callous sentence.

'How much longer will you be able to earn a living from dancing?'

'I'm only in my twenties,' she said indignantly. 'You make it sound as if I'm shuffling around the stage on my Zimmer frame.'

'You're nearly thirty,' Zavier pointed out mercilessly, ignoring her reddening cheeks. 'And furthermore you've been asked to audition for a part that up until this point would have been yours as a matter of course.'

'It's just a formality,' Tabitha spluttered. 'And Aiden had no right even discussing it with you.'

'We're brothers.' Zavier shrugged. 'And it was hardly an in-depth discussion. I just happened to read in the paper about the glut of talent in Melbourne, about the plight of dancers looking for work...'

'I don't recall any such article,' Tabitha retorted, her eyes narrowing. 'And for your information I do read the papers now and then; I'm not a complete airhead.'

'Ah, but my brother is. You're right—there was no such article. But the suggestion of one was all it took for Aiden to sing like a bird, to tell me how hard it was for his dear, ageing Tabitha, how cruel the world of theatre was for a delicate creature like yourself.'

'But why would my career—' she gave a sharp laugh '—or lack of it, interest you?'

'It doesn't.' He tapped the side of his temple. 'You know what they say—knowledge is power. Before that, for all I knew agents could have been clawing at the door to get your signature on a contract.' He held a mocking hand up to his ear. 'Quiet as a mouse. So now

I know how precarious your situation is: you need money, and to boot your work's not exactly secure.'

'I could get a job in an office,' she flared.

'Wearing that?' His eyes ran the length of her body, taking in the ridiculously short skirt, the long expanse of pale, freckled thigh. 'The dress Aiden bought you might see you through Monday, but on your current form I doubt a night at the casino is going to stretch to a full wardrobe.'

'But why me?' Tabitha asked, more to herself than Zavier, her green eyes only finding him once the words hung in the air. 'Why me? Why would you risk your reputation…?'

'My reputation can take it,' Zavier said darkly. 'It would take more than a showgirl with a gambling problem to ruin it. Anyway, marry me and the casino's out of bounds; it's all been taken care of in the contract.'

'Why didn't you ask Amy? It was what she wanted, after all.'

'Because Amy wanted to pretend that love came into it,' Zavier answered irritably. 'Amy wanted the works. You might think this is a big figure, but my *real* wife— the mother of my children—would stand to gain a lot more. With you, Tabitha, it would be entirely a business agreement. You'll walk away independently wealthy and my father will die knowing one of his sons is married and with a tangible hope that grandchildren are on the horizon.'

'Am I supposed to produce a baby?' Her voice was dripping with sarcasm, loaded with scorn. Not for a moment did she expect him to take her question seriously. But again she had misjudged him. Not only did he have an answer; he had it typed up and leatherbound.

'Absolutely not. There will be no children. You might

be happy to gamble your life away, but we're not gambling with the life of a child. I expect you to take adequate precautions, and before you accuse me of being chauvinist, we both know there's an undeniable attraction between us—our previous lovemaking showed no restraint, and certainly birth control wasn't on either of our agendas. I need to know if there have been any consequences from that night before we go any further.'

'Consequences?'

'Are you already pregnant? If you are then that puts an entirely different light on the subject.'

'The deal would be off?' she sneered.

'Let's say it would make things more complicated. Although I wouldn't deliberately put a child into this position, if it's already happened then naturally I'm prepared to stand by my responsibilities and address the issues. So are you?'

Tabitha flushed. Discussing her monthly cycle with Zavier was the last thing she had expected to do—or almost the last, she conceded. Discussing marriage in such businesslike tones hadn't even figured as a distant possibility. But hearing those words—however crudely said, however impossible the dream—hearing Zavier discuss marriage and babies in the same sentence had her senses reeling, her mind wandering, dancing in the delicious faraway realms of impossible fantasies.

Zavier's seed planted inside her. Dark-haired children the image of their father coming from inside her. Zavier's body lying beside her at night, awakening her with its arousal in the morning, the bliss of yielding again and again to his touch.

'Tabitha.' He snapped her back to reality; the surreal reality he had forced upon her. 'Are you pregnant?'

'No.'

'You're sure?'

'Do you want me to pop out to the chemist and buy a kit?'

'That might be the most sensible thing to do, but I'm going to take your word for it.'

Again he deflected her sarcasm; again he floored her.

'I'm sure you will agree that as we will be sharing a bed for the next six months there are bound to be repeats.'

'You're sure, are you?' Her comment was sneering, as if the answer was negotiable, but when Zavier answered she knew her attempts were futile. The fact they would make love again was as inevitable as breathing.

'Positive.' His eyes met hers. He looked so removed from the man who had held her, loved her, but the essence of him still moved her, still made her feel more sexually alive, aware, more feminine than she had ever felt in her life. He wasn't being arrogant, just truthful. Sharing a bed with Zavier and not touching him, holding him, sleeping beside him and not moving her body against him would be equivalent to being told not to breathe for the next six months. Even if she were superhuman, could somehow restrain herself while awake, what would happen as she slept? When the self-imposed barriers slipped and only her subconscious remained, her body would respond to him like a petal reaching to the sun. Her resolve would be dashed the second she closed her eyes.

'I'm asking for six months, Tabitha. Here.'

Snapping her mind back, she realised he was handing her a pen.

'You expect me to sign, just like that?'

'Of course not,' he answered irritably. 'I want to go through the whole document with you. No doubt you're going to demand a few changes, but I warn you I'm no push-over.'

The warning was absolutely unnecessary, but with a jolt Tabitha realised the conversation had shifted. From her initial abhorrent reaction, her absolute rejection of this most preposterous idea, slowly, unwittingly the tempo had changed. It was more a matter of when than if.

How, rather than not.

Her mind reeling, she sat down, trying to ignore the trembling undercurrents as he shifted his chair around the desk so they were sitting side by side, for all the world trying to concentrate on the contract that would change her life.

'We'd be married in four weeks. My family owns a holiday home in Lorne. It's right on the beach, very pretty, and my father has a lot of fond memories and ties to the place. We'll hold the service there, unless of course you're strongly opposed. I don't know if you're religious and would rather get married in a church?'

She looked up at him from under her eyelashes. 'Even if I am, given the circumstances it would hardly be fitting.'

'Good—at least we agree on something.'

With a small wail she flicked through the contract. 'It's twenty pages long. Are we supposed to discuss everything?'

'It's for your protection as well as mine,' Zavier answered, unmoved by her protests.

'Can we at least go out to eat and do it? I'm starving.'

'One thing you'd better realise before you agree to this, Tabitha: you're no longer anonymous.'

She stared at him, nonplussed, and he didn't make any

comment when her teeth distractedly nibbled on the end of his expensive pen.

'The second we become engaged you'll be a Chambers in everything bar name, and this time next month even that detail will be taken care of.'

'Which means?'

'Mess up or play up and, much as you might want to forget about it, there'll be some journalist only too happy to remind you of your misdemeanours. And sitting in a restaurant going through a prenuptial agreement would be over the newspapers in a matter of hours. It's the way it is for us. It's the rule we live by daily.'

'Aiden doesn't,' Tabitha argued.

Zavier shook his head. 'God, are you just a good actress or are you really so naïve? Aiden's scared to cough in case Dad finds out. Why do you think he dragged you along to the wedding? The press have already made a couple of comments about his lack of partner at social occasions—did you really think he wanted you there for your sparkling repertoire?'

'Actually, yes.'

'Please.'

'I know you might find this impossible to fathom, but Aiden actually likes me for me. So don't try and belittle our friendship; that's one argument you're never going to win. I have no doubt if his family were less judgemental and less critical there would have been no need for me to be there.'

A tiny smile was tugging at the edge of his lips, embroiling her in further anger. 'I notice you didn't add "present company excepted" to your little outburst.'

She held his gaze, her tiny face taut and defiant, her eyes wary but with a fire that burned brightly.

'I assure you the omission was intended.'

Even conjugal rights were addressed, right there on page eighteen, with an endless ream of sub-clauses.

Mutual consent…adequate protection…no indicator of the marriage's longevity; the words blurred before her eyes. How could something so beautiful, so intimate, be relegated to a sub-clause in a contract?

Even Zavier managed a small cough of embarrassment as he read out the details. 'I'm sorry, but this had to be put in. As I said, we're kidding ourselves if we pretend it's not going to happen.'

She nodded, a small, sharp nod, not trusting herself to speak.

'It would only complicate things if the legalities weren't addressed now.'

'Of course.'

'Then I think that just about covers everything. Do you have any questions?'

How austere and formal he sounded, as if he had just concluded an interview rather than arranged their marriage.

'Just the one,' Tabitha said with false brightness to hide her nervousness. 'What star sign are you?'

'Pardon.' He looked back at the contract and Tabitha actually laughed.

'You won't find the answer there. We need to know each other's star signs.'

'Why?' he asked simply.

'Because we're supposed to wake up and turn to the horoscope page in the newspaper to find out what the other one's thinking, to find out what sort of day we're going to have, to see if the other's in the mood for romance. You've no idea what I'm talking about, have you?'

For once Zavier was only too happy to agree he was none the wiser.

'One of the first things Marjory will ask is what star sign I am.'

'Of course she won't. It's all a load of rubbish,' he answered irritably. 'I know my mother.'

'I'm sure you do. But she's not only a mother, Zavier, she's a woman, and women do these things. When she asks—which I can practically guarantee she will—if you don't know the answer then an Oscar-winning performance isn't going to save us.'

'Libra.'

'Oh.' The surprise in her voice was evident. Librans were supposed to be warm, loving, tender. 'Were you premature?'

'I was actually on time—to the very day,' Zavier added. 'So what sign are you?'

'Virgo.'

He gave a low devilish laugh. 'Which proves my point: it's a load of rubbish.'

And suddenly there were no pages left. No 'i's to dot or 't's to cross, just a big space for them to sign and date. And as complicated as it was, as intricate as the details were, even Tabitha, with the legal brain of a gnat, understood the gist of the black writing on the wall. She would love him and adore him, in public at least, never embarrass him or jeopardise his status, never waver from the dictated path of the contract. She could have it all— riches, respect, his body, his bed. But there was just one thing the contract left out. One small detail that hadn't been addressed by the nameless lawyers who had created this document.

Love.

The one thing that couldn't be defined, legalised, or rationalised was the only thing missing.

'It's a business deal, Tabitha.' Zavier seemed to sense her hesitancy; his words were surely meant to make her feel better, so why then did her eyes unexpectedly fill with tears?

'I loan out my heart; you pick up my bills?'

'Something like that.' His voice was unusually gentle. Reaching forward, he caught her face in his hand, a heavy thumb smudging away a stray tear that had splashed on her cheek. The surprisingly intimate gesture confused her almost as much as the contract itself. 'But it *is* a good deal, Tabitha. Nobody loses.'

Nobody loses. He watched as a frown flickered across her face. How could he say that? How could he look into her eyes and tell her there would be no losers when six months from now she had to walk away?

'Don't we need a witness?' Tabitha asked, stalling at the final hurdle.

'No,' Zavier said slowly. 'We need time.'

The businessman was back. Clicking into action, he stood up, shuffling the contracts together before tossing them into his briefcase. The strangest thud of disappointment resounded in her chest as she realised he didn't expect her decision just yet, and the thud was coupled with a start of astonishment at her own willingness to sign.

'Sleep on it,' he offered. 'I don't want you feeling forced into anything.'

Picking up the cheque, Tabitha handed it to him, noticing the tremor in her hand as she did so. 'You'd better take this.' She gave a slightly shrill laugh. 'After all, I might just run off with your money.'

But Zavier merely shook his head, refusing the cheque

in her outstretched hand. 'Oh, I don't think there's any need for that.' His eyes narrowed thoughtfully, and though his voice was still soft Tabitha heard the warning note behind it. 'You wouldn't be that stupid, now, would you?' But just as suddenly as the hairs rose on her neck, just as she felt the confines of the contract closing in, heard the warning bells start to ring again, his features softened, an easy smile instantly relaxing his face. 'Come on, you, I'm starving; get dressed and we can go and eat.'

'But I am dressed.' Tabitha shrugged, glancing down at her long bare legs, her pink cleavage spilling out of her wrap-over. 'What's wrong? Don't I make a very good fiancée?'

Zavier laughed, really laughed, and for once it was with real mirth.

'On the contrary, you make a wonderful fiancée. I'm just wondering how I'm going to survive a three-course meal with you looking so appetising.'

CHAPTER FIVE

'WHAT would we tell Aiden?' They were sitting in a sumptuous restaurant, with waiters fluttering like butterflies, filling her glass, placing vast white napkins in her lap.

'You'll tell him nothing.'

Which helped not one iota. Tabitha made a mental note to ring Aiden first thing; the news could only be better coming from her.

'Or tell him an offer you simply couldn't refuse came up.'

'Can I at *least* tell him the truth—that it's a business deal?'

Zavier's eyes narrowed.

'He'll know,' Tabitha insisted. 'After all, it was his idea in the first place.'

'Okay,' Zavier relented. 'But only Aiden. I mean it, Tabitha, no one else can know. Not your best friend, not your hairdresser, not even your parents.'

Tabitha's hands tightened around her glass. 'My parents are both dead.'

If she had expected sympathy she didn't get it. 'Well, at least you won't have to lie to them.'

Shocked at his callousness, she opened her mouth to protest. But Zavier was in full swing. 'No wonder you and Aiden are friends. You're exactly like him.'

'We're nothing alike,' Tabitha protested.

'Oh, yes, you are. Neither of you have ever had to

71

worry about meeting a mortgage payment—no doubt you inherited your house?'

'What on earth has that got to do with anything?'

'Well, it goes some way to explaining why you have such a reckless attitude to money, why you've spent your life to date indulging your fantasies. It must be pretty easy to call yourself a dancer when you don't have to worry about mortgage payments—worry about keeping a roof over your head.'

'You're so bitter,' Tabitha snapped, but Zavier merely shrugged.

'I'm a realist.'

'A bitter realist.'

'Perhaps.' Leaning forward, he lowered his voice. 'We met at the wedding, we fell head over heels in love, we're as stunned as we are delighted.' Tapping his fingers, he reeled off the platitudes then leant back in his chair. 'That's the story we'll tell everyone. No wavering, no deviation—not without discussing it with each other first.'

'Won't your parents find it strange?' Tabitha chewed her lower lip, simply refusing to believe it was all that simple.

Zavier shrugged. 'Why would they? Aiden only ever passed you off as a close friend; it was all innuendo. Just remember: we met at the wedding...'

'...fell head over heels in love...' Tabitha continued as Zavier raised his glass to hers.

'...and are as stunned as we're delighted,' he finished as their glasses chinked. 'Good girl—you're getting the idea.'

Strange that any praise from Zavier made her blush.

'Look, Tabitha, as long as we keep pretending they'll believe us.'

'I'm just nervous, that's all. I can't quite believe it myself; I guess that makes it harder to believe that everyone will fall for it.'

'Why wouldn't they?'

'Does anyone fall in love so quickly?'

For once Zavier was off the mineral water, and he took a long sip of his Scotch before answering. 'Who said anything about love? The fact I'm getting married will be enough for my parents.'

'Speaking of your parents, how are we going to tell them?' Tabitha ventured, but her words trailed off as a beaming, smiling man appeared

'Is everything to your satisfaction Monsieur Chambers?' The owner, obviously thrilled at his clientele, appeared at the table.

'Actually, now you mention it, Pierre, no! Everything is not to my satisfaction.' His haughty upper-class tones filled the restaurant and Tabitha slid down in her chair as every face turned to the impromptu cabaret.

Pierre clicked his fingers and a multitude of anxious waiters appeared. 'What is the problem, *monsieur*? Tell me now and I fix it this instant.'

Zavier's face broke into a smile, and Tabitha's blush only deepened as he reached across the table. Taking her hand, he kissed it deeply, and the coolness of his tongue instantly replaced her embarrassment. In a flash her audience was forgotten as the liquid silk of his eyes met hers, the velvet of his lips slowly working its way over her palm.

'My problem is…' Zavier drawled between kisses, his eyes never once leaving hers.

'*Oui?*' Pierre answered, desperate to please.

'That there's no champagne. Tell me, Pierre, what's

a wedding proposal without your best French champagne?'

It was all clicking fingers, corks popping, bubbles fizzing and congratulations being offered as Zavier dug in his suit, producing a tiny black velvet box.

'I haven't said yes yet,' she whispered furiously across the table, but her indignation at his brazen presumption was brushed aside as he took her hand and closed her fingers around the box, his voice a low drawl and for her ears only.

'You can dump me tomorrow.'

The surprise on Tabitha's face when she fiddled with the tiny gold clasp and the box finally opened was genuine. As the ring caught the candlelight and glittered mockingly in her face she found herself staring at the darkest, largest ruby—beautiful in its simplicity, perfect, even. Everything this relationship wasn't.

'You look surprised.'

She swallowed, then grasped his hand back, aware of their audience. 'Isn't that what you're paying me to look?'

'There's a necklace that goes with it.' He gave a dry laugh. 'I'm supposed to give it to you on our fortieth wedding anniversary.'

As he leant over to whisper in her ear they looked for all the world every bit a young couple in love, on the threshold of the universe with all their lives before them waiting to be lived and loved together. Even Pierre's eyes filled with tears as Zavier pulled her closer.

'This ring is on loan. I'll replace it with one of equal monetary value when the deal's completed. Just don't go getting too attached to it; this stays in the family.'

There was no malice in his voice, no offence meant, just a coolly delivered statement of fact.

The only thing Tabitha had to comfort her was the fact that the tears that inexplicably formed in her eyes had Zavier almost gasping in admiration. 'You're wasted as a dancer, Tabitha; you should try your hand at acting.'

It was only when their main meal had been served and Zavier had waved away the attendant waiters, insisting he was perfectly capable of pouring his own wine, that they started to talk again.

'You still haven't answered my question. How will we tell everyone?'

'That's already been taken care of.'

'You mean you've told them before I've even agreed? Are you so sure that I will?'

Zavier shrugged. 'No to the first; yes to the second.'

She stared at him, nonplussed.

'You'll soon see.'

And despite the initially strained atmosphere, despite the awful lies that bound them, sitting there across the table from him, gleaning tiny details about him, watching his features soften in the candlelight, hearing his voice, his occasional laughter, she saw another side to him. Learnt about the man instead of the icon. Discovered that he could be nice and funny—sensitive, even.

Maybe it was the champagne, the crêpes dripping in dark chocolate and raw sugar. Maybe it was the company. Whatever the explanation, as she sat running her spoon in the rivers of chocolate sauce on her plate, when the bill discreetly arrived in its velvet folder, Tabitha felt like a child watching the Christmas tree being taken down. Automatically she reached down for her bag, ready to pay her share, but as soon as she had done so she immediately righted herself.

Of course Zavier noticed. 'Good girl. You're learning fast.'

Pierre was back, positively beaming. 'I am so delighted you chose my restaurant for this most special night. May I say, Monsieur Chambers, what a beautiful fiancée you have, sir. You make a very handsome couple. Tell me, how did you meet?'

Zavier took her hand before he answered. 'At a family wedding, Pierre. It was only a few days ago, yet I feel I've known Tabitha for ever. She swept me off my feet.'

Pierre clapped his hands together in delight. 'A whirlwind romance. How romantic.'

'Isn't it?' Standing, he offered Tabitha his hand, which she accepted.

As the night air hit them Tabitha let out the breath she had inadvertently been holding. 'Do you think he believed us?'

'Why not? I think we did bloody well, actually. Anyway, Pierre can only benefit, so it's in his interest to believe us.'

'Why?'

He turned, the light from the restaurant enhancing his strong profile, his eyes unreadable. 'You've got so much to learn, little one.'

'But what's Pierre got to do with it? He seemed genuinely delighted at the news.'

Zavier gave a cynical snort. 'Genuinely delighted at the publicity, you mean.'

She opened her mouth to question him further, but before the words even formed in her mind a great weight came upon her, the force of his body literally pinning her against the wall. Her breath literally knocked out of her, all she could do was stare in surprise as his hungry mouth searched for hers, his body pushing, pressing against hers in unbridled passion. Amazingly, she wasn't scared—not for a single second. Even though there was nothing gentle about the way he was holding her, nothing restrained about his searching mouth and hands, the scratch of his chin against her cheek like a million tiny volts coursing through her face.

He tasted of champagne and decadence and danger, his kiss a symbol of the very real danger of the man, the inexplicable thrill of the reckless desire that blinded her. How she would love to resist him, to coolly push him away, but it was an impossible feat. Her hand instantly jumped up, grabbing at his hair, pulling his face closer as she kissed him back deeply. His manhood pressing into her left her in no doubt that he was as aroused as her. For a crazy second she thought he might take her there and then—and what was crazier was that she would have let him. In one swoop he had rewritten her values, the very standards she lived by. Her morals, her inner rules were discarded as she kissed him back. But just as suddenly it was over. He pulled away, barely breathless, triumph blazing in his eyes.

'It's all been taken care of,' he said slowly.

They walked along the river in silence, her face raw and tingling from the weight of his kiss, her body a twitching confused mass of desire. Every few steps Tabitha slowed, lifting her hand to her face, the sheer beauty of the jewel a necessary reminder that she wasn't dreaming.

'Look at that.' The wonder in her voice stopped him momentarily and he joined her as she gazed at the chalking on the pavement. His eyes briefly flicked to the self-portrait, a mirror image of the young artist who sat beside his work, torture in his eyes, the pathetically thin body a mocking reminder of the unjust world in which they lived. An abundance of raw talent reduced to begging on the street. She half expected Zavier to deliver some derisive comment, to pull at her arm, discourage her from lingering; instead, to her infinite surprise, he nodded at the artist.

'This is quite beautiful.' There was no patronising undertone, no superiority, just genuine admiration. 'Can you draw my fiancée?' No price was discussed, no figures traded. Zavier's word was his bond and the young man sensed it, gesturing Tabitha to sit down.

Embarrassed, she wanted to refuse, to walk away now, but it was too late for that. Already bony fingers were sharpening charcoal, those tortured eyes were studying her face, and Tabitha knew that leaving now would probably deny him a meal.

More than a meal, actually.

When Zavier took the rolled-up sheet she watched as he shook hands, then, peeling a large amount of notes, handed them to the artist without a word.

'Can I at least see?' she asked as Zavier motioned her to go.

Briefly he unrolled the work, deigning to give her the briefest of glances.

'It's beautiful.' Tabitha flushed. 'I don't mean *I'm* beautiful, just the drawing.'

'That's talent for you.'

'Aiden sold a painting.' His step quickened at the mention of his brother's name and Tabitha had to half run to keep up with him. 'He's talented as well.'

'Rubbish. Some no-name who probably knows nothing about art happened to buy a picture.'

'Why are you so scathing of him?'

'Because I hate waste,' Zavier spat. 'I hate to see him

throwing his life away, chasing dreams, not facing up to his responsibilities.'

'Why?'

'Why?' He spun around then, his hand gripping her arm. 'Don't you think I have dreams, Tabitha? Do you really think that sitting in an office staring at stock markets is where I want to be every day?'

'But you love your work,' she interrupted.

'Says who? Aiden? My mother?' His eyes flashed and his hands moved in unusual animation. 'They're wrong.'

'Then why do it?'

A small hollow laugh escaped his taut mouth. 'My father put his life into that business, but even when he retired, lucrative as it was, it wasn't going to keep my family in jewels and furs and mansions for the rest of their lives. It wasn't going to keep Aiden in Scotch and designer suits. I've turned it into a bloody empire, ensured my family have carried on living the lives they're used to. If I'd walked away, bummed out like Aiden did, sure we wouldn't have starved—but there wouldn't have been the trappings there are now.'

'So?' Her words seemed to incense him, but Tabitha carried on talking quickly, determined to have her say. 'Money's not everything. I know you think I'm a gold-digger, but I know this much—if you didn't want to do it you wouldn't be there.'

'You mean I should walk away and watch my father's dream evaporate, along with my parents' marriage?'

'Surely there's more to them than just money?'

'Maybe, but my mother has never looked at a price tag in her married life, never thought twice about refurbishing the house, putting in a pool or a tennis court, and somehow I can't quite picture her sticking around if the going gets tough. If Aiden had just met me somewhere in the middle, put in a couple of days a week, maybe we both could have had a life outside the business.'

There *were* two sides to every story, Tabitha realised. Aiden's bohemian lifestyle didn't sound quite so romantic now. Chasing his dream had cost his brother dear, and she could almost see the selfishness in her friend's actions.

Almost.

'He's got talent, Zavier,' Tabitha said urgently. 'It isn't just a dream.'

'Said the dancer to the stockbroker.' His voice was dripping with sarcasm, but Tabitha refused to be deflected.

'I'm a good dancer,' she started slowly. 'But not a brilliant one.' Her hand reached up to his face and turned his taut cheek to face her. 'I can't believe I've just admitted that. I've always kidded myself that one day there'd be that nameless face in the audience, the one that was going to whisk me away, ask me why I was wasting my talent in the chorus line. It isn't going to happen for me. It never was, and that really hurts to say.'

His eyes moved slowly to hers, the pain and honesty in her voice forcing his attention.

'But Aiden... He's got more talent in his little finger than I have in my whole body. His paintings are so beautiful they make me cry. And not just me. You should see them—go to the gallery and look at his display, watch people's reactions when they see his work. You should take your father as well,' she added. 'Maybe Aiden was selfish, chasing his dream, but with raw talent like that I don't think he had a choice.'

Zavier didn't answer. Her heartfelt speech was left hanging in the air, without comment or acknowledgment, and Tabitha could only wonder if it had even registered as he took her arm and they carried on walking. Zavier was so broodingly silent that she knew the end of the night was imminent, that her allocated time slot was over.

With terrifying clarity Tabitha knew that she didn't want it to end.

Idly she stared at the casino as they passed it, watching the huge gas chimneys blasting flames into the air in their half-hourly performance, lighting up the night sky in a huge phallic show of power. But of course Zavier misconstrued her vague interest.

'Is this where your money goes?'

'What? Do you think that I'm going to dash back there once you've taken me home?'

Only Zavier wasn't joking, she realised as he glanced over, a look of contempt curiously interlaced with pity on his face.

'I wouldn't put it past you.' Under the brightly lit forecourt it was as light as midday, but his expression was unreadable. 'Come on, let's go in.'

'I thought it was out of bounds,' Tabitha remonstrated, realising her lie by omission might very easily be exposed once Zavier saw her attempts at gambling. Still, the relief that flooded her at the prospect of prolonging their time together made her protest audibly weak.

'We haven't signed the contract yet. Anyway, if you'd been paying attention you'd know that you're allowed to come to the casino so long as you're with me.'

'But why on earth would you want to bring me here? And why tonight? Is this another one of your bizarre tests?'

'I'm afraid so!' A smile tugged at the edge of his mouth. 'A lot of my clients like to be entertained here when they visit Australia; sometimes you'll be expected to accompany me.'

'Oh, and I suppose you want to be sure I can contain myself, that I'm not going to pull out a pack of cards at the dinner table or descend into a catatonic state at the poker machines in front of your important clients?' She snapped her mouth closed as his grin deepened.

'I think they're a bit too high-rolling for the poker machines. Is that where you spend your time when you're here?'

Tabitha gave a half-nod, consoling herself that at least she was telling the truth—or sort of. Her friend Jessica's hen night had ended up at the casino, and Tabitha had fed a whole twenty dollars into the machines—she was hardly the addict Zavier so clearly thought she was, unless they were talking about shoes!

They were walking through the casino's arcade now, row after row of designer shops, their wares glittering invitingly in the window, their doormen insuring only the truly well heeled even made it past the threshold.

'You know they're expensive when there's no price tag,' she said, pressing her nose up against one of the windows and letting out a low moan. 'Did you ever see anything more heavenly?'

Zavier took in her glittering eyes, the rosy cheeks flushed from champagne and the tendril of red hair cascading from her ponytail and working its way down her long slender neck. He was about to agree when he forced himself to concentrate on the focus of Tabitha's attention.

'It's a pair of black slippers,' he drawled in a bored voice.

'They're not slippers,' Tabitha corrected knowingly. 'They're mules...' She eyed the petite shoes with the cheekiest little kitten heels, the heavily jewelled uppers winking back at her. 'And they're divine.'

'The dress is nice,' Zavier mused, looking at the simple full-length velvet with its shoestring straps. 'It would suit you.'

'But not my bank balance. And, no, I'm not fishing. This is just window shopping, at which I'm an expert.'

'I'm sure you are. Right, where do you want to go?'

Tabitha had no idea, but she took his offered hand and they wandered around for a while. People looking, she mused, would think that we were just an ordinary couple. Stealing a look at her escort, she corrected herself—no, they wouldn't. There was nothing ordinary about Zavier. Such was his aura, his effortless grace, even the most groomed and sophisticated heads turned when he walked past.

She was enjoying herself, Tabitha realised, really enjoying herself. Back at the river she had thought the night had almost ended, the fairytale was over; but here amongst the bustling crowds, clutching her picture, walking beside him, his hot dry hand around hers, in the false day the casino created Tabitha felt that the night might last for ever.

'What are you grinning at?'

'I was just thinking what a good time I'm having.'

'Of course you are. This is what turns you on, isn't it?'

She dropped his hand and stopped walking then. At first he didn't appear to notice, but after a couple of steps turned back.

'What now?' he asked irritably. 'Has a Tiffany ring just caught your eye?'

'I was actually thinking how much better it was when you were being nice to me.'

'Oh.' Zavier managed to look uncomfortable, which gave Tabitha the confidence to continue.

'And if this is going to work, Zavier, surely we should at least try being nice to each other—and not just in other people's company. It's going to be a long six months if we're constantly sniping at each other.'

'Okay,' he mumbled, but Tabitha was on a roll.

'We've already established that where sarcastic one-liners are concerned you're a master, but I for one don't need my faults and shortcomings being constantly rammed down my throat. Yes, this is a business deal, and, yes, if I do accept then I'll come out of this with a huge financial advantage. But you were the one who approached me, not the other way around.'

'Okay, okay,' he snapped.

'That's not being nice,' she retorted.

The champagne had worked its way down to her toenails now, and combined with the undeniable euphoria of finally having an answer to her grandmother's problem it was proving an intoxicating combination. A smart reply, easily as witty as one of Zavier's, was forming, but just as it reached the tip of her tongue a wedge of flesh pushed her against a boutique and he kissed her far too thoroughly, his cool tongue parting her lips like a hot knife through butter.

'Is that nice enough for you?' he growled as she licked her stinging lips, and without waiting for her response he dragged her back into the sea of people.

Tabitha could see how her grandmother's problem had started. The lights, the noise, the hum of the place—the whole extravagant package, actually—gave her a thrill of excitement in the pit of her stomach. Of course the fact she was also on the arm of one of Australia's most eligible bachelors amplified the effect, but Tabitha could certainly see the attraction it must hold for a lonely old woman whose days and nights stretched on endlessly.

Zavier had disappeared to a bar and, after feeding her last note into a change machine, Tabitha took her bucket of dollar coins and settled at a poker machine, trying to assume an air of knowledge as she attempted to locate where to put her money.

Love hearts whizzed around before her eyes, cupid's darts took aim as the machine started singing, arrows flew as dollar signs appeared, and an earsplitting electrical fanfare belted out of the machine.

'Aren't you going to take your free spin?'

He was back, and Tabitha instantly stiffened on her stool, sorely tempted to put her arm up and shield the machine from his sight. But she knew that wouldn't stop Zavier. She could imagine him as a sulky schoolboy, finishing his spelling test first and then peering over with mocking scorn at her futile attempts. And she was positive he was laughing at her—positive at that moment he knew the fraud that she was. Taking her drink, Tabitha pretended to concentrate, pushing the flashing button before her. She could feel the boredom emanating from him and fiddled with the buttons a few more times, watching her credit limit dissolve to zero in two minutes flat.

'So what now?' Turning, she gave him a smile.

'You mean you're already finished?' His eyebrows shot up in surprise. 'I thought we'd be stuck here for hours.' Picking up her bag, he handed it to her. 'Is this your attempt to show me how controlled you can be?'

Tabitha shrugged. 'Something like that,' she muttered, while privately wondering how people could sit for hours staring at the blessed things. Mind you, not everyone had a diversion quite as delicious as Zavier to lure them away. 'Are we going home now?'

He stared at her for a moment, watching as her colour deepened under his scrutiny. 'I thought I'd have to drag you out of here kicking and screaming.'

Mentally chastising herself, Tabitha realised she wasn't exactly behaving like a woman with a gambling problem. 'Sorry to disappoint you,' she said lightly, jumping down from her stool and making to go. But Zavier didn't move. He just carried on staring, his eyes narrowing as he looked at her thoughtfully.

'Come on.' Taking her hand, he led her easily through the crowd and without a further word led her up mazes of escalators until the thronging masses eased off. Suddenly the fairground-like, carnival mood of the casino had evaporated; suddenly they were back in Zavier's world. The world of the well dressed, with dimmed lights and discreet music, a world where doormen greeted you by name and *never* asked for ID, where even the bar staff never thought to charge.

A world away from Tabitha's.

A vast wooden door was opened as if by magic, and Tabitha blinked a couple of times as the heavy cigar smoke that filled the air reached her eyes.

'Why have you bought me here?' she asked slowly, terrified he might ask her to play one of the tables.

'To teach you a lesson.' His hand was still wrapped around hers, and he pulled her nearer but didn't bother to drop his voice. 'The minimum bet here's a thousand dollars. I'm going to show you just how easy it is to lose money.'

'Oh, come on, Zavier.' She turned to go but his hand gripped hers ever tighter. 'There's no need for this.' She let out a nervous giggle. 'I gamble away the odd twenty dollars or so; this is the big league.'

'It's all relative.' His eyes narrowed. 'Anyway, I'm not the one in debt here.'

'Well, you might be soon.' Tabitha gestured to the tables. 'Look, Zavier, this has gone too far...' She had to tell him, had to stop him—everything was getting way out of hand. 'I don't have a problem with gambling. I don't know how you got the idea—'

'So you're suddenly cured?'

'I never had a problem in the first place—'

'Save it,' he snapped.

'But I don't—'

'You see that guy over there?' This time his voice did drop. 'Hands clenched, sweating buckets?'

Tabitha followed his gaze, nodding as she saw the unfortunate gentleman who was now fishing a large silk handkerchief out of his undoubtedly expensive suit. 'I bet if you asked he'd tell you that he hasn't got a problem either. Yet he probably just lost his house, or his car, maybe his business, and no doubt he lost his wife a while back. And see that woman there? The one in the green dress?' He didn't wait for her response. 'See how she's chewing on her lip, taking a drink every few seconds? Well, if she had any sense then she'd get the hell out. Like I said, it's all relative, whether it's twenty dollars or twenty thousand. If you can't afford it you shouldn't be here.'

Despite her awkwardness Tabitha listened, enthralled, his insight was amazing, his descriptions spot-on. 'And I suppose you'll just stand there calmly?'

'That's right.' He led her over to a soft low sofa and they sat down, drinks seemingly miraculously appearing before them before the waiters discreetly melted away. 'I'll set my budget and stick to it.'

'Oh, very controlled,' Tabitha said sarcastically. 'It must be hard, being so perfect all of the time.'

'Hey, I thought we were being nice to each other.'

'We are,' Tabitha grumbled. 'Except when you start lecturing me.'

'I'm not lecturing you. Well, maybe a bit,' he admitted. 'But it's for your own good. The difference between us, Tabitha, is I know when to stop.'

'Fine,' she snapped, nervous at the thought of him gambling money to prove an extremely unnecessary point. 'You do what you want. Just don't expect me to join you.'

'So the poker machines are more your thing, then?' His upper-class accent was mocking now. 'You don't fool me, Tabitha. The only reason you don't want to join in is because you don't know how to play the tables.'

'Look,' Tabitha said very definitely, her hand pulling at his suit sleeve as he turned to go, 'I don't have a gambling problem.' She allowed him one long bored sigh before tentatively continuing. 'I really don't. The debt you heard Aiden and I discussing is my grandmother's… I hardly ever come here!'

He didn't look at her. Pointedly removing his sleeve from her grip, he took a long sip of his drink before finally turning to face her. 'Then why the sudden euphoria, Tabitha? Why the flushed face and the sparkle in your eyes? The second we walked in here I could feel your excitement—feel it,' he reiterated. 'So if it isn't the casino that's doing it for you, why the sudden change?'

'Zavier!' She almost shouted his name, but he didn't even blink. 'Why do you think I'm so excited? It's not every day a girl gets a marriage proposal. It's not every day…' Her voice trailed off, and from the shuttered look in his eyes she knew she was wasting her time; a word like love simply didn't factor in here.

'You've got a problem,' he snapped. 'You can deny it all you like, but the only person you're fooling is yourself, Tabitha.'

Sinking back into the sofa, Tabitha nursed her drink. 'Oh, I've got a problem all right,' Tabitha muttered as he stalked off towards the table. 'Six foot four's worth.'

She didn't have to worry about her cover being blown. She could take a full-page ad out in the papers telling him about her grandmother and he'd still just put it down to denial. But why had she let him think she had a problem in the first place? Surely a gambling addict was hardly a flattering light to put oneself under? Looking over, she watched him. Not a muscle flickered in his face, not a single bead of sweat marred his brow. His brief nod at the croupier was friendly and relaxed. Turning momentarily, he caught her eye.

'All right?' he mouthed, and Tabitha nodded, a strange feeling suddenly welling in her. Despite his protests, despite his attempts to prove otherwise, Zavier Chambers was a nice man.

His back was to her now, but she could just make out his strong steady hands moving a pile of chips across the table. The woman in green was taking another nervous sip of her drink as Zavier stood unmoved next to her. She watched the woman walking away, tears in her eyes, shaking her head in disbelief at her loss. Perhaps the magnitude of what she had gambled was only now starting to dawn.

She could end it all here—walk away now and have lost nothing. It was Tabitha taking a nervous sip of her drink now, her hand tightening around the glass as she mentally rolled the dice.

Standing, she made her way over, one hand gently touching Zavier's shoulder as she quietly observed the game in progress.

'I thought this wasn't your scene?' Zavier turned briefly as an inordinately large pile of chips was pushed towards him.

'It seems you were right after all,' Tabitha murmured, breathing in the heady scent of him as she edged just a fraction closer, feeling the solid warmth of his legs against her barely clad thighs. 'Maybe I don't know when to stop.'

CHAPTER SIX

'THANKS for the lesson, by the way.' Tabitha let out a gurgle of laughter as his car pulled up outside her house. 'You've definitely cured me.'

'I'm never going to live this down, am I?' Even Zavier was laughing as he pulled on the handbrake. 'I couldn't have lost my car keys tonight if I'd tried; I made a bloody fortune. So much for trying to show you the error of your ways.'

'Lesson well and truly learnt,' Tabitha answered in a solemn voice, then broke into hysterics again.

'You're a bad girl,' Zavier said gruffly, and something in his voice stopped her laughter. Something in the way he turned his head, his dark eyes glittering in the moonlight, made Tabitha's heart-rate accelerate alarmingly.

'Maybe I am, but I make great coffee.' Running her tongue nervously over her bottom lip, she watched his hands tighten on the steering wheel. 'Do you want to come in?'

'Better not.' His words were clipped, and Tabitha felt the good mood of earlier evaporate, steaming up the car window as she sat there suddenly void of anything to say. The tension in the air was palpable. 'It's been a good night, though.' His voice was strained, forced. 'I really enjoyed myself.'

'Don't.' The single word was out before she could stop it, and it hung in the air as she forced herself to continue. 'I mean, you don't have to pretend now; I know you're just being nice.'

For an age he stared at her. 'I thought nice was what you wanted, Tabitha.'

'It is….'

'Well, then, don't complain.' He nodded to the house. 'You'd better get inside. The neighbours' curtains are starting to twitch.'

'How did you know where I lived?' It suddenly dawned on Tabitha that he had taken her home without direction, and her mind reeled from impossible scenario to scenario. 'Did you have me followed? Have you been watching me?'

'Nothing so exciting, I'm afraid. I looked you up in the phone book.'

'Oh!' She let out a nervous giggle and Zavier smiled, but the drumming of his fingers on the steering wheel indicated her allocated time slot was over.

'When will I see you again?' It came out wrong, needy and unsure, and his idle drumming on the steering wheel stopped momentarily. 'I mean, what do we do now?'

'That's up to you.'

'So I passed the test back at the casino?'

A smile skated on the edge of his lips and Tabitha ached, ached to put up her fingers, to catch the glimmer of light in his tired, jaded face.

'You passed,' he said simply. Leaning over to the passenger side, he pulled the contracts from his briefcase, then flicked on the car light. She watched, her breath hot in her lungs, as he scrawled an extravagant signature on each of the documents before handing them to her. 'Drop them off at my solicitor's if you decide to go through with it.'

'That's it? That's all I have to do?' The simplicity of the action truly terrified her.

'That's it.' Zavier shrugged. 'Look, I really am going to the States tomorrow, to close off some deals. Anyway, it will be easier that way—playing the part of the devoted fiancé for the next month or so might prove a bit too hard. I'll ring you with all the details once I've worked things out, and my driver will pick you up, take you shopping for the wedding and take you to Lorne. In the meantime keep your nose clean. I'll be in touch.'

'But surely I have to do something. What about invitations, my wedding dress…?'

'It will all be taken care of.'

And with that she had to make do. Stepping out of the car, she half expected him to call her back, to pull her into his arms, to end the perfect evening in the perfect way. But he didn't—just sat there watching as she let herself in.

She watched from the darkened lounge window as his car slid off into the darkness, the ring on her finger heavy and unfamiliar.

Unable to fathom what had just happened, the enormity of Zavier's proposal only now truly registering, she expected to be awake for hours, to lie in the darkness staring at the ceiling, wrestling with her conscience. But for the first time since the wedding Tabitha fell into a deep and dreamless sleep, as if seeing him had somehow stilled the restlessness in her soul.

Only when the sun arose, when the trucks in the distance shifted their gears noisily and schoolchildren chattered excitedly outside her bedroom window as they passed by on the way to school, did her sleepy eyes open as the door below was pounded.

Her mind was whirring, the ring still heavy on her finger, her mouth dry from the champagne, her heart hammering as the previous night's events repeated themselves.

Surely it was a dream—a strange, vivid dream? Surely it could never have happened?

Wrapping a robe around her, she pulled the bolt on the door, half expecting to see Zavier telling her it was a joke—a mistake, perhaps.

'Delivery for Miss T. Reece.' A huge white box was thrust into her arms, and as she wrestled to hold it and somehow sign the delivery note her heart-rate quickened as Aiden made his way purposefully up the garden path, his grim face a million miles from the gentle man she loved and knew.

'What the hell have you done?' Ignoring the delivery boy he burst past, slamming the door as she stood there in the hallway. 'Page four,' Aiden practically spat, flinging the morning paper at her. 'The headline reads "Marriage made in Financial Heaven".'

Shaking, she put down the box and struggled with the newspaper, a small gasp escaping her lips as she turned the pages. There she was—at least, there her hands were—lost in Zavier's hair, the glint of the ruby on her finger, the searing memory of his kiss immortalised in a photo now.

Aiden grabbed back the paper, reading it aloud in a taunting voice. '"Met at a wedding! Swept off his feet! A whirlwind romance!" My God, Tabitha, what have you agreed to?'

Pierre must have rung the press the second the first champagne cork had popped. So that was what Zavier had meant when he'd said it had all been taken care of.

'I haven't agreed to anything,' Tabitha answered quickly, playing for time.

'That's not what it says here,' Aiden snarled. 'Do you want me to carry on reading?'

'I was going to tell you,' she begged. 'I was going to ring you this morning.'

'To tell me what, exactly? You mean this is all true? You really are marrying him?'

'I don't know…'

'It was Zavier you were with the night of the wedding?'

'How did you know I was with anyone?' She was stalling, dreading the questions her answers would lead to.

'I got up to get a glass of water—you know, mouth like a carpet and all that. I never said anything at the time because I figured it was none of my business. But if it was Zavier you were with then I'm damn well making it my business.' He was struggling for control now, and Tabitha stood speechless as he hurled the newspaper at the wall. 'It was him you were with, wasn't it?'

She nodded, staring dumbly at the carpet, unable to meet her friend's eyes.

'I told you not to get involved. I warned you about him. Honestly, Tabitha, he's no good for you. He may be my brother but he's still a bastard.'

'He's not. Honestly, Aiden, we went out last night and he was really nice…' Her voice trailed off as she recalled Zavier's shuttered eyes in the car.

'Can't you see that he was just being nice because you were doing what he wanted?'

'Of course I can.' Tabitha swallowed hard, hating the fact but knowing it to be true.

'You're going to get hurt, Tab.' He was nearly crying now, and Tabitha wasn't far off herself. 'You're going to get so hurt.'

'How can you be sure?'

'Because I know him. Why, Tabitha? How did you get into this? And please don't quote the newspaper—I need to know what's happened?'

'He offered me money.'

'*I* offered you money.'

'He offered me more.'

Aiden refused to buy it. 'I know you, Tabitha, as well as, if not better than, I know Zavier. I offered you enough to get your grandmother out of debt and a bit more, and yet you refused.'

'It's a lot more than you offered,' she admitted, shame filling her. 'A lot more.'

But still Aiden steadfastly refused to believe her. 'He could have offered you the Crown Jewels and you'd have turned him down.' Sitting on her sofa, he stared moodily out of the window. 'You love him, don't you?'

'This has nothing to do with love.'

'Bull.' He practically spat the expletive and Tabitha winced. Seeing Aiden so angry was something she hadn't reckoned on. 'You love him, and you're hoping in time he'll love you too.'

'Of course I don't love him, Aiden. I hardly know him.' But the uncertainty in her voice was audible even to herself.

'That didn't stop you sleeping with him,' Aiden pointed out nastily. 'Just what the hell's going on between you two, Tabitha? And don't feed me this line about money; I just won't believe it.'

'There is an attraction,' Tabitha admitted slowly, unsure how to explain what she couldn't even articulate to herself. 'But I'm not stupid enough to believe a marriage can survive on sex alone. It's a lot of money, Aiden. It will change my life. I can open up my own dance school.

Yes, you offered me money and, yes, you offered me marriage. But, Aiden, how long would it have lasted? How long before we'd be exposed? At least this way...'

His eyes locked on her hand, his face growing more incredulous by the moment as he lifted it up and examined the ring. 'He gave you the ruby?'

'It's a loan,' Tabitha said breathlessly. 'He made it very clear he wanted it back.'

'He said he'd never let it out of his sight again.' Aiden's voice was one of utter amazement. 'Swore on his own life the next time a woman wore that ring it would be the real thing.'

'The next time?'

Aiden looked up at the question in her voice. 'He was engaged a couple of years ago, to this sweet young thing—or so we all thought. Two weeks before the wedding Louise went and got herself some hot-shot solicitor to draw up the most complicated prenuptial agreement, figuring that Zavier wouldn't back out of the wedding at that late stage.'

'And did he?'

'Yep.' Aiden gave a wry grin. 'The one thing she didn't bank on when she worked out her plan was Zavier's exacting standards. The day he realised it was more about money than love he dropped her—and there was nothing dignified about Louise's exit, let me tell you. Even as we speak there's a court action against him for breach of contract and emotional trauma. But this isn't about money,' Aiden insisted again through gritted teeth. 'You can deny it all you like, Tab, but this *isn't* about money. You know it and so do I.'

She did know it, yet was too terrified to admit it— even to herself. 'He thinks the gambling debt is mine.' Watching his uncomprehending face, Tabitha took a breath before venturing further. 'I tried to tell him the truth but he just refused to hear it. Please, Aiden, don't tell him otherwise.'

'He'll find out anyway,' Aiden was shouting again. Tabitha put her hands over her ears but he carried on relentlessly. 'Hell, he probably already knows. He's using you, Tabitha. You can't win this one.' He quietened then, his voice softening when he saw her pain, saw the tears coursing down her cheeks. 'It's not too late to say no. Your surname's not in the paper. Zavier can shoot the rumours down in five minutes flat—he's done it for me before... He'll demand a retraction and it will all be forgotten. You won't need to go through this ridiculous charade.'

Which was what terrified her the most.

Tabitha closed her eyes. 'Please don't hate me, Aiden. I couldn't bear it.'

'I don't hate you, Tabitha, I'm just scared for you— for me too, come to that.'

'What have you got to be afraid of?'

'You're my best friend, Tabitha, and he's my brother. I don't want to lose either of you, and when it all goes bad—as it surely will—I don't want to have to choose.'

There was so much finality in his voice, such a jaundiced air of inevitability, that the gnawing sense of foreboding she had awoken with multiplied with alarming speed and a surge of panic swelled within her.

'It won't come to that.' Her voice wavered and there was nothing assured about her response.

'I hope not.'

'Will you give me away?'

'You're going to go through with it, then?'

'*If* I do go through with it,' Tabitha corrected, 'will you give me away?'

Aiden let out a low whistle. 'You're pushing it, you know?'

'Please, Aiden. I'll be nervous enough; at least I won't have to lie to you, pretending to be the blushing bride and all that. You know it's just a business deal.'

'But is it?'

She nodded, slowly at first and then more certainly. 'You know it is. Please, Aiden, I really need you to be there for me.'

He stared at her for a moment. 'Okay, then, but I'm not buying you both a present. I'll save my money for the mountain of tissues and chocolate I'll undoubtedly have to dole out when it's all over.'

'I'll be fine,' Tabitha said resolutely. 'I know what I'm doing.'

'I hope so,' Aiden said simply, and, giving her the briefest kiss on the cheek, he let himself out.

Only when she was alone did Tabitha remember her parcel. Her hands still shaking from the confrontation— from everything, really—it took for ever to open, but as the box slid open she let out a gasp of delight. The dress and shoes she had admired so lovingly last night lay on a mountain of tissue paper, only they weren't black. Instead the softest, palest lilac beckoned her hands, which she ran over the soft velvet of the dress. In a second Tabitha's robe was discarded and the dress skimmed over her head. Slipping the shoes onto her feet, she searched through the tissue paper until she found what she was looking for.

It wasn't quite the declaration Tabitha had secretly been hoping for, but just the sight of his purple signature somehow soothed her.

Funny that a hastily written note with a noticeably absent kiss gave her more pleasure than several thousand dollars' worth of clothes, Tabitha thought as she sat there dressed in all her finery staring at the piece of paper.

'Six months,' she whispered to herself.

Six months of sleeping beside him, waking next to him in the morning. Six months to show Zavier how good and sweet love could be if only you let yourself taste it.

Six months to make him love her.

In a corner? Maybe.

Making a mistake? Probably

Taking the biggest gamble of her life? Definitely.

Of course there was never a pen when she needed one, but a rummage down the side of the sofa finally delivered the goods, and with a shaking hand Tabitha held the contract and added her signature beneath Zavier's— not quite with flourish but with definite determination.

There were a million reasons she should have said no to Zavier, and only one truth. The simple fact that she loved him was the real reason Tabitha said yes.

CHAPTER SEVEN

'WE'VE put you in here.' Marjory Chambers flung open
the shutters. 'I know you and Zavier will probably think
it old hat, but until you're married at least I've put you
in separate rooms. Jeremy wouldn't hear of anything
else.' Marjory gave her an engaging smile, misinterpret-
ing the look of relief that flooded Tabitha's face as she
pointed to a door. 'Of course the rooms are adjoining,
so what you get up to is your business.'

Everything about today felt surreal. She expected
grandeur after the wedding, but the Chambers holiday
home was practically a mansion. There was nothing dark
and stately about it, though. Wall-to-wall floorboards,
huge white walls littered with black and white photos,
sumptuous white leather couches and artefacts each mer-
iting more than a cursory glance. If this was their holiday
home heaven only know what their main residence must
be like. Her bedroom jutted out onto the ocean, its vast-
ness glittering before her, the bay view to end all bay
views.

'Jeremy's having a lie-down, but we'll be having
drinks on the patio at seven before dinner. He can't wait
to say hello. But please, Tabitha, feel free to come down
before then—make yourself at home. I know this last
month can't have been easy on you, with Zavier being
away, but it's over now, he'll be here within the hour
and finally we can get on with this wedding. Now, do
you want me to look after your dress? Zavier simply

mustn't get even a glimpse; you're going to look stunning.'

Marjory was so nice, so disarmingly friendly, that as Tabitha unzipped her suitcase—new, of course—and passed her the wads of tissue paper that contained the lilac dress and shoes Zavier had sent her, she was suddenly assailed by the biggest wave of guilt.

'I brought you these chocolates.' She hadn't known what to bring. What did you give to someone who'd got everything? No doubt there was a cellar bursting with the finest wines, which had ruled out anything Tabitha could pick up at the local supermarket, and anticipating gardens trimmed and manicured to perfection had made flowers seem rather paltry. So she had settled for chocolates—wasn't that what everyone did? And not the usual half-kilo slab that she occasionally treated herself to. Tabitha had splurged on the best she could find in the department store. They had cost a small fortune; hopefully she'd get a taste!

Thrusting the package at Marjory, Tabitha felt a blush spread over her cheeks.

'I didn't know what to get.'

She was taken back by the sparkle of tears in Marjory's well-made-up eyes.

'Oh, Tabitha, you're such a dear thoughtful girl.'

Tabitha shuffled her feet. 'I know it's not much.'

She was enveloped in a hug within Marjory's heavy scented bosom. 'They're perfect, and so are you…' Her voice trailed off as the sound of tyres crunching on the gravel broke the moment.

'Aiden is here!' Marjory exclaimed, but the excitement she reserved for Zavier was noticeably absent. 'I must go and welcome him. Won't you come down?'

Tabitha politely declined; another lecture from Aiden

was the last thing she needed right now. 'I'll stay and unpack, if you don't mind.'

'But the staff will take care of that.' Marjory's voice softened then. 'Silly me. You'll want to spend some time getting ready for Zavier.'

As Marjory rushed from the room Tabitha set about unpacking, and finally, when every last thing had been put away, when she had fiddled with her hair long enough and rouged her cheeks, sprayed scent over every inch of her body, there was nothing else to do. Nothing but wait with mounting trepidation for the crunch of gravel that would bring her future husband to her side. Since the day she had met him, since the day he had burst into her life, knocking her sideways with his sheer presence, he had dominated every facet of her life. As surely as any major trauma he had inflicted more drama, more emotion than she had ever experienced to date. Though her days had been filled with work, with time spent sorting out her grandmother, explaining her sudden wedding to her stunned friends, the practicalities had been a breeze compared to the torturous mental abacus that had overwhelmed her: counting the weeks, the days, the nights, the hours until she saw him again.

She felt him approaching before the low snarl of his engine was even audible. A cynic would say it was guesswork—after all, his plane landed at four, the timing was inevitable, perhaps her subconscious heard him without realising—but she knew as sure as her heart was beating that there was something deeper going on here, some mental telepathy that had invaded her. This very moment had sustained her through the uncertainty of the last few weeks, but now that the moment had actually arrived she was completely overcome with nerves, and the all too familiar sense of foreboding, Zavier randomly triggered, assailed her again. She was playing with fire here, and someone was bound to get burnt. Tabitha held her breath, standing just far back enough from the open window so she couldn't be seen.

Perhaps she moved, maybe a shadow fell, but whatever the reason he lifted his head, his eyes searing into the room in which she stood. Ducking backwards, Tabitha caught her breath; she knew he hadn't seen her, knew it was impossible, but there was no safety in logic.

Trembling, she sat on the bed, berating herself for the impossible situation she had thrust upon herself. She wasn't just messing with her own life here; she was playing Russian roulette with every person in this house. How was she going to face him? How was she going to look at him after all these weeks and not betray what was seared in her heart?

Love wasn't in this equation.

Yet.

'Tabitha!' The happy shriek from Marjory made her jump. 'He's here!'

Painting on a smile, she made her way out of the bedroom, reaching the top of the stairs as Marjory pulled the front door open.

Tabitha had hoped that the passage of time would somehow diminish his beauty, that the man who stepped gracefully into the entrance hall would hold only a distant charm. That she could play along with the charade and still keep a semblance of control.

She was wrong on all counts.

His beauty literally knocked the breath from her, and she stood there stunned as his eyes slowly lifted to hers, her breath coming out in short bursts, her nerves snapping to attention, deprived for so long and only now awakening as the master returned.

'Don't I get a welcome home kiss?' he drawled.

Slowly she made her way down the stairs, but as she reached the last couple the violence of her desire, the magnetism that surrounded him, made her literally run into his arms. It was him she needed, his strength was all that could get her through, and she fell into his arms and he pulled her close and kissed away the salty tears that had unexpectedly sprung from her eyes.

'Hey, I'll have to go away more often if that's the welcome I get.'

Embarrassed at her emotive display, she kept her head trained on the floor.

'Don't you dare,' Marjory scolded. 'You have to learn to delegate, Zavier. You're going to have a lovely wife to come home to now; you can't be jetting off at a moment's notice.'

'Someone has to work,' Zavier quipped.

Tabitha wasn't a big drinker, but never had she been more grateful for the gin and tonic Marjory thrust into her hand. Taking a large sip, she sought some refuge as the sharp taste hit her tongue.

'You look stunning, Tab.' Aiden finally acknowledged her, squeezing her hand and taking a hefty sip of his own drink as he did so.

She knew it must have been hard for him and she smiled gratefully, happy they were friends again.

'Every bit the bride-to-be.'

She almost felt it.

This whole week had been spent in a frenzy of preparation. Her legs being waxed, eyebrows tweezed, eyelashes dyed, shopping for bathers and cocktail dresses. Zavier's driver had indeed picked her up and taken her shopping. Had handed her a credit card with a discreet nod and a list of instructions that would have caused most women to think they'd died and gone to heaven. The driver had waited outside the most exclusive shops as Tabitha searched amongst the beige and navy suits and fitted dresses for the lilacs and pinks and moss-greens she adored, the velvets and silks that were so much her own style, so much more readily available at the craft markets she frequented. Filling smart bright bags with designer labels, exclusive one-offs, she had felt sick at what she had so effortlessly spent.

Good money after bad.

The weight of her deception was almost unbearable.

'Where's Dad?'

'Asleep.'

'How is he?'

Marjory flashed a perfectly lip-lined smile that every-one in the room knew was false. 'He's doing very nicely; he's just tired, that's all. He'll join us for dinner; now let's go and have a huge drink.'

'Let's not,' Zavier drawled. 'I think I'll take Dad's lead and have a lie-down.' His eyes flickered to Tabitha, who stood there suddenly deflated. What she had ex-pected from this the strangest of reunions she had no idea, but it came as a huge anticlimax that now she had finally seen him he was disappearing so fast.

Just what did you expect? she scolded herself. That he'd be pleased to see you? But her spirits lifted as he pulled her close, running a lazy hand around her waist. 'Perhaps you could bring me up a drink.' He kissed her then, again, and this time it was absolutely unnecessary, for no one had doubted the joy in their reunion.

This blatant display of sexuality Tabitha knew had been entirely for her benefit, and the thought simulta-neously thrilled and terrified her, making even the sim-plest task of pouring a Scotch a feat in itself. Knocking gently, she quietly opened Zavier's door. The drapes were drawn and she stood there for a moment, allowing her eyes to become accustomed to the darkness. Making her way over, she passed the heavy crystal glass to him; the touch of his fingers made her jump and most of the contents of the glass trickled between their fingers.

'Steady. You're really nervous, aren't you?' Zavier observed.

'Terrified,' she admitted.

'Why? They all believe us. Even Aiden seems to be coming round to the idea.'

'Good.' Her voice was strained; she was scared she might reveal it wasn't his family that was unnerving her at the moment, wasn't the charade they were playing, but the impact of him close up that terrified her. 'How was America?'

'Great—didn't you get my postcard?'

Which ended that conversation. Zavier would no more write a postcard than fly to the moon. He had propped himself up on one elbow, and, placing his drink on the bedside table, he pulled his tie looser.

'You must be exhausted?'

'I've spent sixteen hours sleeping on the plane.'

'Oh, that's right.' Tabitha gave a wry laugh. 'There was me feeling sorry for you, imaging you slumming it in economy, but no doubt you flew first class—or does your family have its own private jet?'

'No, but for heaven's sake don't suggest it or it will be on top of Mother's list of "must haves".' It was a tiny joke but it made her smile, though it wobbled slightly as his finger came up to her lips.

'That's better. I forgot how beautiful you look when you smile.'

He was being nice to her, gentle and funny, and she

didn't know how to respond, didn't know what was real any more.

'Lie beside me.'

'Why?'

'Practice. We're going to have to get used to sharing a bed, and anyway I don't like sleeping on my own.'

And no doubt he never had to, Tabitha thought, but she was weakening. 'I shouldn't.'

'Why?'

Tabitha swallowed. 'Your mum put us in different rooms; it wouldn't be right.' She was fighting for excuses. Marjory had practically opened the adjoining door for them, handed her consent on a plate, but it wasn't some delayed moral code that was preventing her lying down beside him. It was the very real fear that she might weaken and tell him how she was really feeling. Tears were threatening, and the emotions of the past few weeks, the desperate need to see him, the fact he was actually here, the shock of his tenderness were all doing unimaginable things to her self-control.

'Come here.' They were the same two words he had used on their first night together, the same two words that had catapulted her into his arms, and this time the effect was gentler but just as devastating. Slowly she unstrapped her sandals, before stretching out on the bed beside him.

'We mustn't…'

'I know.' He pulled her into the crook of his arm and she lay there rigid, her breath hot and bursting against her lungs. 'How has it been, the last few weeks?' She didn't answer, just lay there, revelling in his embrace. 'How did your family take it?'

'There's only my grandmother.'

'So how did she react to the news?' His voice was so

deep, so soft, it was almost lulling her to sleep as she lay in the darkness next to him.

'She was surprised, pleased, stunned—the same as my friends, really.'

'Why were they surprised?'

Wriggling slightly, she turned in the darkness towards him. 'Well, the speed of it. They all initially tried to convince me that I'd gone crazy. I guess there's not many people left who believe in love at first sight. How about you?'

'What about me?' He was half-listening, half-asleep.

'Do you believe in love at first sight?'

'There's no such thing as love.'

She stared into the darkness, waiting for him to finish his sentence, waiting for him to elaborate. When he didn't, when the only sound that reached her ear was his gentle rhythmic breathing and the ticking of his watch, she realised he had finished talking. 'You don't believe in love at all?'

'I believe in lust, compatibility, friendship—but love like in the movies? There's no such thing, Tabitha.'

'But of course there is.' Propping herself up on her elbow, she jabbed him playfully in the ribs, but Zavier was deadly serious. Taking her hand, he pulled her back into his arms.

'There's no such thing,' he repeated. 'I thought I'd been proved wrong once, actually thought I'd hit the jackpot.' His voice was detached but Tabitha could feel the tension in him as he spoke, and she listened intently, desperate for insight, for understanding. 'For a while there it was great, but it was just a fantasy, like one of your fairytales. Louise never loved me. Sure, she was attracted to me—liked me, even—but that's not the type of love you're going on about.'

'Just because it didn't happen with Louise it doesn't mean there isn't someone out there for you.'

He gave a low laugh. 'The other half that will make me whole? You've been watching too many films, Tabitha. I'm telling you there's no such thing.'

His words tore through her—to hear him so cynical, so scornful, defied explanation.

'I know Louise hurt you, Zavier, but to write off the rest of the human race because of one bad relationship— surely that's a bit of an overreaction?'

'It isn't an overreaction. I can't think of one marriage in my entire family that hasn't been about money.' He lay there, thoughtful for a moment. 'No, not one—ours included.' He gave a loud yawn, stretching his body languorously beside her, his arms reaching above his head then wrapping back around her. 'Funny, I actually missed you while I was away.'

Stunned, scared to move in case she had somehow misheard him, Tabitha swallowed hard.

'You missed me?' Her voice was a whisper and she finally turned to him, but Zavier didn't answer. His eyes were closed, his mouth slightly open, the sulky look on his face even in sleep. She went to get up, to go to her own room and somehow glean some breathing space, somehow try to add up all the pieces that were Zavier. But, grumbling, he pulled her back, his arm clamping down around her, his face burrowing in her hair with a low moan, and she lay there scared to move, in case the spell was broken.

If this was the hell she was destined to for her sins then Tabitha could take it. Pompous, arrogant, scathing he might be, but the occasional glimpse of what she believed was the real Zavier made up for it all tenfold.

Surely something that felt so right, so natural, couldn't be *all* wrong?

CHAPTER EIGHT

SHE dressed at lightning speed for dinner, terrified that the intimate mood might somehow evaporate while he showered. But out of his arms, as she pulled on a pale lemon shift dress and strapped on her sandals, the demons that constantly sniped at her returned.

Of course he was being nice; he wanted this to work as much as she did, and keeping her on side was one way of ensuring that their audience remained convinced.

Walking down the stairs, he took her hand, and as they entered the lounge his grip tightened. They joined the group and it took only one look for Tabitha to realise that the sudden strength of his grip wasn't about lending her moral support.

Jeremy Chambers sat in a wheelchair. He seemed light years away from the powerful man of just a few weeks ago, his face haggard and thin, his eyes sunken, but his suit was impeccable and there was an air of dignity and strength about him that illness couldn't ravish, no matter what else it took.

'Tabitha.' He took her hand, kissing it gently. 'You look stunning.' He winced slightly as he let her hand go.

She knew he was in pain, but instinct told her that Jeremy didn't want his pain to be acknowledged.

'We're thrilled to welcome you to our family.' He turned to his son, hesitating slightly as he caught his breath, even the minimal exertion of greeting his future daughter-in-law a huge feat in his poor health. 'How are you, son? How was America?'

No flip reply for Jeremy, Tabitha noted. Instead Zavier plunged straight into an in-depth report, reeling off figures as if he was giving a presentation. It was almost inhuman, the knowledge his brain held. Not once did he ask his father how he was feeling, and the wheelchair was dismissed as if it had always been there. Tabitha knew that was exactly how Jeremy wanted it, his face rapt as he listened to his son intently.

'Bores the hell out of me.' Marjory rolled her eyes. 'But just look at Jeremy—it's exactly what he needs: a bit of intelligent conversation. I admit I'm as guilty as anyone. The second he sits in that damned wheelchair I find myself speaking to him louder and even answering for him.'

Tabitha smiled sympathetically at her honesty. 'I'm sure you'll all get used to it.'

'Let's hope we have time to.'

'How are you feeling, Dad?' Aiden's awkward attempt at conversation brought nothing more than a frown and a sharp retort from his father, and Tabitha reflected how austere and formal Jeremy sounded when he addressed his younger son, how sad that it had come to this.

'So, how are the wedding preparations going?' Aiden forced a smile and walked over to the more receptive audience of his old friend.

'I've no idea,' Tabitha admitted honestly.

'Don't tell me—' Aiden grinned '—everything's being taken care of.'

Tabitha laughed at his perception. 'Apparently all I have to do is turn up.'

'Nervous?'

She nodded, relieved at finally being able to be honest with someone.

'What does your grandmother say about it all?'

'She's as stunned as everyone else.'

'Is everything sorted there?'

She went to take a sip of her drink but realised that her glass was empty; instead Tabitha picked up the lemon slice, sucking on it, she gave a small nod. 'For the time being.'

Aiden lowered his voice. 'She needs help—you know that. You mightn't have done her a favour, getting her out of trouble again.'

Tabitha was down to the pith now, but that was more preferable than talking about her grandmother's problem.

'Gambling's an illness,' Aiden continued relentlessly. 'It doesn't just go away. The debt might be cleared but it will just mean the bar's raised higher next time.'

'There won't be a next time,' Tabitha replied indignantly.

'But that's exactly what you said before,' Aiden reminded her. 'And the time before that, if I remember rightly. How can you be so sure that this time things will be different?'

'Because next time the bailiffs come knocking there mightn't be a multimillionaire prepared to bail me out.'

'It's those little things you say that make me love you more.' Zavier slipped an arm around her waist, but there was nothing tender about the kiss he placed on her cheek.

She had meant her words for Aiden only, in defence of her grandmother, her brutality a cover-up for the genuine fear she felt for her only real family, and knowing Zavier had heard made her stomach sink. Sure, they both knew it was a financial arrangement, but the gentle acceptance, the truce she had demanded, was undoubtedly over.

'And for your information, *sweetheart*—' his lip curled around the word '—it happens to be a billionaire bailing you out. But then what's a few more zeroes to a dizzy thing like you? What's a few million here or there when you're prepared to blow your last cent on the poker machines?'

'What are you lot looking so serious about?' Marjory was all smiles, wagging a finger as she joined them.

'We were just discussing my fiancée's little *problem.*' He arched one perfect eyebrow as Tabitha stood there mortified. He wasn't going to mention it? He couldn't—not here!

'What problem, Zavier? Do tell.' Marjory giggled, moving closer. 'Anything that needs a woman's viewpoint? I'd be only too happy to help.'

'You wouldn't know where to start,' Zavier said ominously to his mother, and Tabitha held her breath. 'Unless that is, you've taken a crash course in domesticity all of a sudden. Tabitha's glass has been empty for the past five minutes and no one's bothered to fill it. You really need to have a word with the staff.'

The ringing of the bell summoning them for dinner was the only thing that made Tabitha remember to breathe again.

Dinner was awful.

Oh, the food was perfect, the wine delicious, the conversation scintillating, but dinner really was awful.

Zavier studiously avoided her eyes, and the hand that briefly brushed hers was icy cold. Any headway that had tentatively been made was now seemingly dashed by one inappropriate comment.

The conversation inevitably turned to the wedding,

and Tabitha struggled to concentrate, to laugh at the right moments, to inject some enthusiasm into her voice when she listened to what Marjory had in store for them.

'I've put all the gifts that have arrived so far into the drawing room; we'll have to decide where we're going to display them. It's a shame you didn't want a bridal registry—you've doubled up on a couple of things.'

'How many toasters?' Tabitha's feeble joke fell flat on its face as Zavier leant back in his chair.

'None—well, I can only vouch for my side of the family anyway. Mother, just how many toasters have we received from Tabitha's side?'

'Just ignore him, darling.' Marjory giggled, not remotely fazed by the simmering tension. 'I do believe he's getting nervous. How about you, Tabitha?'

'A bit.' That was the understatement of the century, but unlike Zavier at least she was trying to sound as if she cared. 'Still, at least it's just a small wedding. I couldn't cope with much more than that.'

'The only problem with that...' Zavier's sardonic drawl at least momentarily forced the attention from Tabitha '...is that I've a feeling my mother's version of "small" might differ somewhat from yours. Isn't that right, Mum?'

Marjory clapped her hands gleefully together. 'Well, I can't promise small, but I can guarantee it will be tasteful.'

Zavier rolled his eyes, but smiled affectionately at his mother, and Tabitha noticed how much nicer he looked when he addressed someone he truly loved. Gone was the haughty menacing expression she was becoming so used to, instead his face seemed softer, younger, perhaps, and infinitely more desirable. 'Why don't I believe you? No doubt you've already put in an order for heaven only knows how many helium balloons and a couple of ice sculptures.'

'No,' Marjory said defensively. 'Balloons are old hat now. I'm sticking with fresh flowers.'

'Good choice—and how many ice sculptures?'

Tabitha had thought he was joking, but her face dropped a mile when Marjory shuffled uncomfortably. 'Just the one.'

The groan that escaped Tabitha's lips was muffled by the guffaws of laughter around the table, though Zavier caught her eye as she sank lower in her seat. For the tiniest second he smiled sympathetically, and she knew then she was forgiven. For that brief instant she was privy to a glance from him that wasn't suspicious or malicious, and for all the world it felt like a caress. What was it about him? It was as if he had a hotline to her soul—one small look could wrap around her like a warm blanket on a cold night. She felt the colour in her cheeks mount under his watchful eyes, even managing a small smile back.

Maybe Marjory's ice sculpture wasn't such a bad idea after all, she thought. At least it might cool her down, though the heat that was radiating from her now would melt it in a flash. Clearing her throat, Tabitha dragged her eyes away, smiling around the table.

'Marjory, it's such a lovely night—I wondered if I might take my port out on the balcony?' The vast dining room seemed stifling now, and the need to escape the oppression of her lies overrode Tabitha's usual shyness around the Chamberses.

'Of course, my dear, make yourself at home. It can get rather warm in here.'

Gratefully Tabitha picked up her glass and made her way through the French windows onto the balcony.

It was a beautiful night; placing her glass on the stone wall, she rested her arms and gazed at the magnificent view. The bay shimmered before her, dark indigo as deep as Zavier's eyes but with flashes of silver as the moonlight hit the waves. The endless water glimmered in parts, and she imagined the couples entwined on the dance floors, sharing romantic meals in the bayside restaurants.

She envied them.

Envied them for the uncomplicated lives they must surely lead compared to hers. Envied these unknown people for the gift of requited love.

'You seem miles away.'

She had half expected him to join her; in some ways she had engineered it.

'I was over there, actually,'

Her slender arm lifted and she pointed to a cluster of lights sparkling on the foreshore.

There was no need for further explanation. He seemed instinctively to understand how her mind had wandered.

His eyes followed to where she was pointing. 'And were you enjoying yourself?'

Tabitha laughed. 'Actually, no, the food was terrible.'

'I'm sorry for earlier.'

She swung around, visibly stunned; never in a million years had she expected any sort of an apology from him. If anyone should be apologising it was her.

'Sorry for what?'

'For making you so uncomfortable before dinner—pretending I was about to reveal your gambling problem. It was a cheap shot, not my usual style at all.'

'I'm sorry too,' she admitted. 'What I said to Aiden—I didn't mean...'

'Yes, Tabitha,' he said slowly. 'You did.'

She didn't say anything; instead she reached for her drink, taking a hesitant sip, confused at the change in his demeanour.

'But it didn't give me the right to put you on the spot. We both know it's business; I guess sometimes it's all too easy to forget. We must be good actors. Unfortunately you seem to bring out the worst in me. Or the best in me. I guess it depends what night we're talking about.'

His eyes almost imperceptibly travelled the length of her body and she knew he was remembering not just what had happened but every last searing detail. Knew that as his eyes flicked to her breasts Zavier was tasting her all over again, that when he glanced at her feet, confined in the strappy summer sandals, he was remembering her undressing, the feel of her thighs wrapped around his solid torso...

Swallowing the port she was holding in her mouth, Tabitha resisted the urge to rush over to him, to bury her face in his chest and feel his arms tightly around her.

That night, that one stolen, decadent night. She had brought out the best in him. Oh, Tabitha wasn't the world's greatest lover—lack of experience put paid to that—but they had both brought out the best in each other. Their lovemaking had been wondrous—divine, even—and the memory of his touch, the gentleness she had glimpsed, gave her the confidence to broach a question.

'Doesn't it make you nervous?'

'What?'

Her hands gestured as wildly as her eyes; she couldn't believe he didn't know what she was talking about. 'This. This lie.'

He shook his head. 'Why should it?'

'What if they find out?'

'They won't—at least so long as you show a touch more discretion than you did with Aiden earlier.'

'But what if they do?' Tabitha insisted.

'Then I'll deal with it. Anyway, the Chamberses aren't going to collapse because of another loveless marriage in the family. My father just wants me married; he never said anything about love.' He was so confident, so arrogantly assured it annoyed her. Suddenly she wanted to see him squirm, wanted Zavier Chambers to admit to even a tenth of the fear that gripped her.

'What if I don't turn up? What if I just disappear with your money?'

His eyes narrowed. 'I'd soon track you down. It was a generous amount but hardly enough to disappear on. Anyway, no doubt it's already spent.'

'But isn't this eating you up inside?' The anguish in her voice was evident, and Zavier looked at her thoughtfully before answering.

'Look, Tabitha, you remember those people at the casino—sweating buckets, chewing their nails, clutching their chips, willing themselves on? I'm not like that.'

'You'd set your budget,' Tabitha reminded him, not sure where the conversation was heading. 'You could afford to lose.'

'Okay, then, take work. Every day I make billion-dollar deals, shuffle money. Whether it's a gamble or an educated bet, I roll the dice every day, but the difference is that I can walk away. I'm not like the rest of the guys I work with—compulsively watching the stocks, swallowing ulcer tablets, imagining the worst. They'll be burnt out by the time they're forty, strapped to a cardiac monitor on the coronary care ward and wondering what the hell went wrong. Me, I'll still be playing this game when I'm seventy.'

'So where's the analogy?'

His face broke into a grin. 'What on earth are you talking about?'

'Well, I'm assuming there is one. I'm sure this short sharp lecture on the exigencies of stocks and options is leading somewhere. I do read the business pages now and then,' she added as he muffled a cough. 'I don't automatically turn to the horoscope page.'

'Ah, but *I* will now.' He laughed. 'I can hardly wait to find out what's in store for me tomorrow. You were right, actually. My mother did ask what star sign you were.' His voice hardened then. 'Don't threaten me with mind games, Tabitha; nothing fazes me. If you're there then we'll get married—great. If you're not I'll survive.' His face was menacingly close, his voice a silkily disguised threat, but despite his foreboding stance, despite her trepidation, the adrenaline that coursed through her system had nothing to do with fear.

She could feel the warmth of his body, his breath on her cheek, his eyes pinning her to the wall behind. There was nowhere to go, nowhere to run and absolutely no desire to do either. The air was crackling with sexual tension as his hand brushed her arm. The tiny hairs stood up and her nipples jutted through the fabric of her dress, painfully greeting their master.

'We get married in two days.' Her tongue moistened her lips nervously, and she knew the innocent gesture had aroused him. 'Maybe we should wait.'

'Is that what you want?'

It wasn't. Right now all she wanted was to be in his arms, for him to take her upstairs and for the skill of his lovemaking to obliterate the endless conundrums in her head, for him to take her to a place far away from the problems of the surreal world they had created. Picking up her hand, he ran it across his face, burying his mouth in it. She could feel his tongue running along her palm, working slowly along her life line, then up her wrist. Her knees were trembling; she was sure at any moment she might faint with longing. Suddenly he pulled her hand down to his groin. With a start she felt the weight of his arousal through his dark suit, angry and fiery under her fingers. He pushed her hand still harder against him.

'Someone might see,' she gasped, trying to pull away, but his vice-like grip only tightened.

'It's too dark outside for them to see.' He was pushing her hand against him and he let out a low groan as her fingers moved independently, tightening around the velvet steel of his manhood. She was stunned at her own boldness, berating the clothing that separated their searing skin.

'That analogy you wanted,' he whispered. 'I've made my bet; I've narrowed the odds.' His hand pushed hers deeper into his groin. 'That,' he growled, but there was a breathless edge to his voice, 'is the reason you'll be there.'

His wicked eyes grinned mockingly into hers as she angrily pulled her hand away. 'Who knows, Tabitha? You might be the world's first bride to get there early.'

CHAPTER NINE

HER body ached with fatigue. Most of the night she had lain on tenterhooks, painfully aware of Zavier just a few feet away, aching for him and yet simultaneously dreading him coming into her room; wanting him to, yet terrified he might. Finally she had drifted into an uneasy sleep, only to be awoken what seemed like moments later by the sun. For a while she lay there, taking a moment to orientate herself. The lapping of the ocean was so close she felt as if she might reach her hand out of the bed and touch the cool water. How peaceful it all seemed, how serene compared with reality, with the Pandora's box of lies they all were living. One wrong step, one misguided comment and the whole festering mess would burst forth.

Not that Zavier seemed bothered. Did nothing upset him? Did nothing worry him?

Slipping on some shorts and a T-shirt, Tabitha pulled some runners onto her bare feet. Creeping slowly through the darkened house, sliding the bolt, she slipped quietly out onto the driveway.

She had no direction, no purpose behind her steps, but instinctively she made her way to the beach. Slipping off her runners, she walked a while, trying to fathom the hows and whys, the impossible puzzle that was Zavier, until finally, with a moan, she sank to the soft sandy floor, the damp sand cool against her bare thighs, the lapping waves tickling her toes, rushing in up to her knees, skimming the top of her cotton shorts before being pulled back to the ocean, back to where they belonged.

He saw her first. Sitting there alone on the deserted beach, the rising sun catching her Titian locks, setting them on fire, her long limbs blending in with the water. She looked like some exotic surreal fantasy, an auburn mermaid washed ashore, cast out from the ocean and into the chaos of life on land.

Last night his façade had slipped. Despite what he had said he hadn't slept on the plane, and that had been a bad idea. Whisky and jet lag were a dangerous mix, a lethal cocktail that had, for a moment, blinded him to what she was about, had made her seem appealing, tempting. She wasn't a mermaid, she was a vixen—stealing her way in, menacing and dangerous—and it would serve him well to remember the fact. His face hardening, Zavier picked up his pace, running directly towards her.

He watched her face turn, the set of her slender shoulders stiffen as she realised it was him, wariness filling those stunning jade eyes.

Bewitched, yet not in the way he had expected. The passion from before was gone; the calculated moves of yesterday had all evaporated. More bewitching, more achingly appealing, was the undisguised depth of despair in those calcite pools, and, gazing into them, Zavier found himself breathless, as if he had run the length of the beach and back.

'Couldn't sleep, huh?'

She shook her head, drinking in his presence. Dressed only in a pair of faded denim shorts, his hair for once tousled, he was unshaven, unkempt, but infinitely desirable.

'Pre-wedding nerves?'

She forced a small brittle smile. 'Something like that.'

As he lowered himself beside her the beach seemed to implode around them, and Tabitha moved sideways a fraction, as if making room for him to join her.

A silence followed, but it wasn't painful. They both drank in the stunning view, the endless curve of the bay, watching the liquid gold reflections to their right as the rising sun hit the ocean, the pier filled with fishermen, the waves dotted with surfers, taking advantage of the early-morning swell, riding the waves with skill and precision mixed with overwhelming abandonment, in tune with nature. Tabitha fought to focus, to stem the tide of lust his mere presence summoned. And when the silence had stretched on too long, when something finally had to be said, it was Tabitha who broke it, saying the second thing that came to mind.

The first would have been her undoing.

'I wonder if it's like working in a chocolate factory?'

'Sorry?'

'Apparently, if you work in a chocolate factory they let you eat as much as you want. After the first few weeks of gorging yourself, sooner or later you get sick of it.'

'I'm still not with you.'

'This—' She gestured to the ocean. 'I wonder if you lived here whether one morning you'd open the curtains and not notice the view; if you'd become blasé about it?'

He nodded his understanding. 'God's own country, isn't it?'

The sun was up now, the red and gold hues that had filled the air over till the next time. The sky was blue, dotted with tiny wisps of white cloud that would surely burn away within the hour. The beach was no longer deserted. Joggers were starting to appear, and the occasional dog, diving into the sea, retrieving sticks, swimming with pink tongues lolling, seemingly grinning at the splendour of it all.

'Morning, Zavier. Good to see you back.'

An elderly couple walked over to them, their wrinkled hands entwined, an air of peace and contentment about them. Zavier greeted them warmly, introducing her as his fiancée. The pride in his voice fooled even Tabitha for a moment.

The gentleman smiled at her curiously. 'We actually read about it in the paper. We're so pleased for you both. And may I say, Zavier, what marvellous taste you have. The newspaper certainly didn't do your bride justice.'

'The wedding's pretty much family, really, but it would be great if you could come and join us for a drink afterwards.'

'We'd love to.' A dog bounded up to them, dropping a stick, his breath panting from joyous exertion. 'I think we're being summoned. We'll look forward to Saturday, then.' Picking up the stick, the man tossed it into the air before taking his wife's hand and ambling on along the beach.

'There's your answer.' Zavier's voice echoed her own thoughts. 'They're here every morning—at least every morning that I've been here, for the past thirty years or so.' His eyes were squinting as the sun hit them, sparkling now, his teeth white as he smiled, more to himself than to her. 'Every time they tell you what a great morning it is. Rain, wind or shine, they're walking hand in hand, loving every moment.'

'Loving each other,' Tabitha said slowly.

It dawned on her then: she had always known she wanted him, adored him—loved him, even—but the full magnitude of her love hit her then, as her eyes flicked down to her hand, down to the gleaming ruby on her ring finger. It wasn't just the ruby ring she wanted; it was the necklace and the forty years that came in between. To walk along the beach hand in hand with him every morning, their children running ahead.

And later, when the lines around his eyes had deepened, when the jet of his hair was sprinkled with silver, when it was grandchildren playing at Zavier's feet, vying for his attention, she wanted so much to be there, wanted her past to be bound to his, their legacy to last.

Wanted to be the one.

'Why the pensive face?'

She swallowed hard. How could she tell him that she loved him? Always had. That from the second he had walked into the church, into her life, his name had been indelibly scored into her heart. How could a man whose life was run by fact, deadlines and contracts understand something as simple, yet as inexplicable as love?

But how could she not?

The crashing of the waves swirled in time to the pounding in her temples as Tabitha fought for eloquence, struggled to articulate what was written in her soul. 'There's something I need to tell you.'

'Sounds serious.'

His flip remark only unnerved her further; the magnitude of her feelings truly terrified her. 'It is.'

Despite the heat of the morning Tabitha suddenly felt chilled to the bone. Telling him now would surely change everything. Zavier wanted a woman he could discard with ease when the allocated time slot was over. Love wasn't on his agenda, and telling him now might end everything. It was a business deal, for Zavier at least, and a declaration of love could only spell the end, but her back was to the wall now and something needed to be said. 'I don't have a gambling problem.' Okay, so it wasn't the big one—fireworks didn't suddenly start whizzing through the air and cupid's dart might have missed its mark for a moment—but if Tabitha couldn't tell him what was truly in her heart right now, she wanted at least a semblance of honesty between them.

If her revelation was somewhat an anticlimax Zavier didn't notice. He let out a low hiss. Rolling onto his back, he stared up at the sky, his eyes squinting in the glare before he snapped them closed. 'I don't want to go into it again, Tabitha. We've already covered that.'

'But I don't—'

'So you keep saying. I can't make you admit it—it has to come from you.' He let out a low laugh. 'I've been reading up on it.'

His eyes remained closed, effectively shutting her out, but Tabitha carried on talking, her voice breathless. 'I've tried to tell you. It's my grandmother that has the problem.'

'Well, thank God I covered babies in the contract; your affliction must be hereditary.' His eyes were still closed, his voice a sarcastic bored drawl. 'You'll be telling me it's not your fault soon.'

'You don't understand.' He wasn't making this easy. Zavier's absolute refusal to accept the truth had Tabitha wondering if it was even worth it, yet suddenly it was imperative she tell him this. If he couldn't know that she loved him, she at the very least needed to walk up the aisle with as few lies between them as possible. 'I've never had a problem, and if you won't believe me— keep refusing to listen to me—then I can't go through with tomorrow.'

His eyes flicked open. Rolling onto his side, he eyed her slowly as she stared fixedly ahead. 'Does Aiden know?'

She gave a small, hesitant nod.

'So why the hell didn't he tell me?'

'I asked him not to.' Her voice was a strained whisper, her eyes screwing tightly closed as she struggled with his questions. 'Anyway it probably didn't seem relevant at the time whom the gambling debt belonged to.'

'Didn't seem relevant?' For the first time ever she heard Zavier raise his voice. She had seen him angry, livid, even, but always, always in control.

Until now.

Black eyes were blazing at her, a muscle leaping in his cheek, his neck and shoulders absolutley rigid with tension.

'Didn't seem relevant,' he repeated. 'I'll tell you why it didn't seem relevant—this is just another one of your lies, another one of your…'

'It's the truth, Zavier.'

Her small voice did nothing to stop the tirade, and still he steadfastly refused to believe her. 'At the casino…' his hand was on her chin now, jerking her head around, forcing her to face him. 'You were suddenly so alive, so vibrant.'

So in love.

Still her eyes were screwed shut. How could she look at him and lie about the one thing that mattered? But if she wanted to keep him, wanted her shot at paradise, lying was her only option. 'It had nothing to do with the casino, Zavier, nothing at all. If I was suddenly happy it was down to the fact I had the best part of a bottle of champagne inside me and more than a few years' wages in my bag with a promise of more to come. Is it any wonder I felt so good?'

It was the hardest thing she had ever done, the most vile lie of all, and if she hadn't been so wrapped up in her own angst maybe she would have registered the pain in his eyes, the drop of his hand from her chin as he sat there in silence.

'I'm sorry,' she stammered when Zavier didn't say anything. 'I thought you'd be pleased.' Unshed tears sparkled in her eyes, the aftertaste of her words still bitter in her mouth. 'Pleased that I wasn't a gambler.'

'What? Were you expecting a round of applause? Some noble little speech about what a wonderful woman you are, saving your grandmother from the loan sharks with no thought for herself?'

Tabitha looked up sharply. 'No. I just thought it would help us if you knew the truth.'

'The truth is that this is a business deal.' His words were harsh, angry. 'I don't care about your grandmother—or you either, come to that—so save the little speeches, Tabitha. Save the guilt trip and the dramas. The only person getting worked up about this wedding is you. And as for the gambling debt, you were right—who it belongs to isn't relevant.'

She shot a look at him from under her eyelashes. 'Isn't it?'

'You cashed the cheque the day after you got it,' Zavier pointed out. 'What you spent it on is your business, so long as it was within the confines—'

'Of the contract.' She finished the sentence for him. 'It was.'

'Fine,' he snapped. 'So unless you come up with the money by tomorrow you owe me, Miss Reece, big time. The contract still stands.' The anger left him then, and, propping himself on his elbow, Zavier looked at her thoughtfully. 'Any other little gems you want to toss at me? Any other truths you'd like to share while we're being so open?'

His voice was laced with sarcasm. Tabitha managed a brief shake of her head, biting on her lips to stop the tears.

'So nothing's changed, then?'

'I guess.' Her long fingers were dragging through the sand, drawing endless swirling circles in the virgin smoothness.

He watched her, his eyes slowly dragging the length of her body. Her toes were still painted the same shade of coral they had been at the wedding. Her legs were slender and long, pale freckles skimming the translucent skin, her thighs toned yet soft on the underside. The same legs that had been wrapped around him; the same legs that had pulled him closer, driving him on, pulling him deeper. Suddenly Zavier was hit in the groin with a burning longing, and the searing memory of the soft warm flesh against his skin was so vivid his hand unthinkingly crept closer, his fingers absently stroking the soft marshmallow of her thigh, the need to feel her, to touch her, surpassing all logic.

Tabitha turned abruptly. She had been lost in her own world, oblivious of his mental lovemaking, but as his fingers made contact she jumped, her body tremulous, shocked eyes widening despite the glare of the sun, her pupils constricting against the bright light till the pools of calcite seemed bigger than the ocean.

'What are you doing?' It was a pointless question, one that didn't merit an answer, and he rolled towards her, pinning her to the soft beach, a quilt of flesh and muscle bearing down, burying her with hot needy kisses that almost drowned out reason.

Almost.

With a sob of frustration, of anger, she wriggled away, the tears that had threatened dangerously close now.

'You've just told me you don't care about me, just sweetly reiterated that this is business, and now you have the gall to kiss me, to touch me. This isn't just business, Zavier, and you know it as well as I do...'

He gave a low laugh. 'This is the pleasure. I never said we couldn't mix the two. In fact you signed yourself up for it, remember...'

In one lithe movement she pulled herself up, but he was too quick for her, grabbing at her ankle. He held his hand there in a vice-like grip as she stood, and when he was sure she wasn't about to make a bolt, when the rigid muscles relaxed slightly, he loosened his grip, working his hand slowly up the length of her freckled leg, toying with the top of her shorts. She felt her groin contract, a bubble of moisture welling between her legs.

'This was very much a part of the deal...'

She stared back at him for the longest time. The fact she wanted him was a given, and to deny it would be a lie, but right here, right now, she also hated him. She had told him about her grandmother, her darkest secret, her deepest pain, and he hadn't even graced her with a decent response. She had been right not to tell him of her love, Tabitha acknowledged with relief, and until that ring was safely on her finger she had to be sure he didn't realise her truth.

'You think this is pleasurable?' Her voice was steady, her lips white, and she stared down at his hand with a sneer. 'You think I'm enjoying this?'

For the first time she saw a flicker of doubt in his eyes, felt his grip loosen on her ankle. Freeing her leg, she shook her head ruefully. 'You think you're such a bigshot? Well, I've got news for you. It's business for me too. The only pleasure I get from you is cashing your cheques.'

'You want me as much as I want you.' The words were assured, his voice laced with his usual haughty tones, but she knew she had thrown him; that tiny flicker of doubt still darted in his eyes.

'You once accused me of being a good actress, Zavier. Perhaps for once you actually read me right.' And, turning on her heel, she ran the length of the beach, not once looking back, determined he would never see the tears that coursed down her cheeks or hear the sobs that rasped from her lungs.

She knew, had she stayed one moment longer, he would have seen the truth in her eyes.

CHAPTER TEN

'HERE they are,' Marjory gushed as they stepped out onto the patio. 'We were just about to send out a search party. How long does it take to get changed for lunch?'

'Sorry.' Reaching over, Tabitha planted a long kiss on Zavier's rather taut cheek, determined to keep up the act despite the most unwilling partner. 'I take full responsibility—don't I, darling?'

Marjory's giggles in no way made up for the black look Zavier threw at her, or the visible wince as her lip brushed his cheek, as if her touch was more than he could stomach.

'Where's Jeremy?'

'Oh, Jeremy's gone for a siesta—probably conserving his energy for tonight's dinner. He's not a fan of the sun—not now, anyway.'

A glass of something long, cold and delicious appeared in front of her and Tabitha took a grateful sip. Only the smarting of her eyes and the warm feeling as it reached her stomach told Tabitha that the drink wasn't as harmless as it looked.

Lunch was hell. The man who sat beside her on the patio was positively brimming with anger, not a trace of indigo in the black coal chips of his eyes. Of course the fruity little number Aiden and Marjory were knocking back meant that his sarcastic comments, his biting repartee and dark looks for the most part went unnoticed. If ever Zavier had been foreboding, brooding, unnerving, to date it had only been a dress rehearsal. The row that had ensued back at the house had been of such humongous proportions it would probably rate a mention on the six o'clock news, somewhere between nuclear missile heads and urban warfare.

And in a perverse sort of way Tabitha had enjoyed it.

Enjoyed the confirmation that Zavier Chambers wasn't completely unflappable, that underneath that ruthless, pitiless shield beat a mortal heart, and questioning his sexual prowess made it bleed. Of course the fact that he was more of a lover than Tabitha had ever imagined, that the very thought of him made her toes curl in anticipation, didn't even rate a mention; why ruin a good thing? Zavier's fury she could almost deal with; it was the truth that could hurt her the most.

By the time lunch was over Aiden had long-ago given up on the fruity number and had worked his way down the neck of a bottle of Scotch—which left more for Marjory. Only Zavier carried on with his mineral water, his eyes never leaving Tabitha, making her acutely aware of her every movement, making every delicately prepared mouthful like sandpaper in her throat.

'This time tomorrow you'll be husband and wife.' Marjory beamed, pushing her untouched dessert aside and signalling for a refill. 'I bet you're so excited, Tabitha.'

'I wouldn't bet on it,' Zavier drawled. 'Apparently looks can be deceiving—can't they, darling?'

Fortunately his below-the-belt black humour was far too subtle for his family, who carried on smiling as Tabitha slid further into her seat.

'Well, I don't know about you lot—' Marjory's voice seemed to be coming at her through a thick fog '—but

I'm going to work off my excesses in the pool. Won't you join me, Tabitha?'

'I'd love to, Marjory,' Tabitha answered in a falsely bright voice as she replaced her napkin on the table with a slightly shaking hand. 'But I'll just watch from the poolside for now. I've eaten so much I'd no doubt sink like a stone if I ventured in the water.'

Thankfully, Marjory's plans to work off her lunch weren't quite so energetic as they had initially sounded. Flopping onto a huge sunbed, she snapped her fingers impatiently at one of the staff and they brought over yet another tray of drinks. Tabitha shook her head as the tray passed her. 'Not for me, thanks. I'd love a mineral water, though, please.'

'You sound like Zavier—him and his water. Come on, Tabitha, have a proper drink.'

'I'd rather not.' A loose tongue was the last thing she needed at the moment. 'I'm not a big drinker, especially during the day. And anyway, I want to look my best for the wedding.'

That seemed good enough for Marjory, and she smiled affectionately as Tabitha slipped out of her dress down to her skimpy yellow bikini—four triangles and shoelaces really—painfully aware of Zavier removing his shorts and T-shirt, every hair on his body, every glistening toned muscle seeming to taunt her with its beauty.

'Do you fancy a swim?'

Mute, she shook her head, remembering the last time he had undressed in front of her. She felt his eyes skim over her and dared to dream he was remembering the same.

The two women watched in amicable silence as Zavier dived into the vast pool in one lithe motion, streaming through the water, his muscular body hardly making a ripple as he parted it. There was no way on earth she'd get in now, Tabitha decided. Her doggy paddle was nowhere near his élite level, and there was far more chance of looking graceful on land than thrashing about in the water.

'Don't let Zavier's mood upset you.' Tabitha looked across startled, surprised Marjory had even noticed. Marjory was carefully examining her face in a large hand mirror while simultaneously smearing vast quantities of sunscreen around her eyes and over her décolletage. 'He's just worried about his father.'

Tabitha didn't answer. No doubt Zavier *was* worried about Jeremy's increasingly fragile health, but she knew his black mood was due to a rather more basic problem.

'We're so glad he found you,' Marjory continued, her eyes never once leaving the mirror. 'I know how difficult he can be, and to be honest we were worried for him.'

'In what way?' She was treading on dangerous water here; insights into Zavier weren't part of the deal, but they were way too tempting to pass up.

'Well, he's so exacting. It's all black and white to him. You know about Louise, I presume?'

Tabitha nodded. 'The girl he was engaged to?'

'Lovely thing—though not as gorgeous as you, of course. She even managed to loosen him up a bit—you know, get him out of a tie on weekends and things. They'd have been so happy, but she messed it up, the silly girl—got too greedy. The day Louise came home with that prenuptial agreement it was all over bar the shouting. He'd never admit it in a million years but she really hurt him.'

'No wonder,' Tabitha responded thoughtfully. 'It's hard enough finding someone to spend the rest of your life with without being filthy rich and wondering if they're just with you for your money.'

'Oh, *please*, Tabitha, money matters. As much as I adore Jeremy, I wouldn't have given him a second glance if he weren't wealthy. Life's hard enough without worrying about money.'

Tabitha blinked a couple of times; even though Zavier had told her, she was utterly stunned at the blatancy of Marjory's revelation.

'But you seem so in love.'

'We are,' Marjory tinkled. 'I'm merely saying our relationship would have been a complete non-starter if Jeremy hadn't a bean to his name. Come on, Tabitha, are you honestly telling me that Zavier's money doesn't influence you in the slightest?'

It was a strange question—and, given the fact it was coming from Zavier's own mother, even more confusing. No wonder he was so mistrusting. She had thought Zavier was being his delightful cynical self when he had said that Marjory was with Jeremy for the money, but here she was, openly admitting that money came first and love a poor second.

'I...' Tabitha didn't know how she could answer. After all, money *was* the only thing binding her and Zavier; it was money that had brought them to the eve of their wedding.

And it was money that would end it.

Tabitha pondered before answering. Dreaming for a moment the impossible dream, dreaming that Zavier loved her. She knew one thing for sure: if he lost everything it wouldn't matter a scrap so long as they had each other. Broiled on the passion of her imagination, Tabitha was at least able to answer the question with conviction.

'Money shouldn't come into it. Marriage should be

about love, taking the good times with the bad, leaning on each other, growing together...'

The slow handclap resounding behind her made Tabitha stop in full flood.

'Bravo.' Dripping, he sat on the sunbed next to her. 'Did you hear that, Mum? Doesn't that little speech restore your faith in the human race?'

'Gorgeous, isn't she?' Marjory agreed sleepily as she lay back and closed her eyes, totally missing the venom behind his words, oblivious of the scorn in her son's eyes. 'Darling, put some oil on Tabitha. That fair skin of hers is going quite pink already. We can't have her looking burnt for tomorrow.'

'I can manage myself.' Hastily Tabitha reached for the bottle, but Zavier was too quick for her.

'Don't be silly. You're as red as a beetroot. Lie down.'

Without making a scene Tabitha was left with no choice but to do as she was told. Her eyes met his; swallowing nervously, she stared at him like a rabbit caught in headlights. He seemed to sense her fear, and the malicious glint in his eye evaporated, the dewy hues of lust softening the black weight of his stare.

'Lie down,' he repeated, but this time his voice came out in a husky caress.

Nervously her eyes darted to Marjory; she was sure she must surely sense the crackling sexual tension. But Marjory was dozing, soft snores coming from her slack lips, and with the tiniest nod of acceptance Tabitha rolled onto her stomach, holding her breath as he fiddled with the gold clasp of her bikini.

The oil was already warm from the hot Australian sun, and as he squeezed it onto her skin the chill she had anticipated didn't eventuate; instead she lay there as the slippery moisture seeped onto her back, jumping only when his cool wet hands came into contact with her rosy skin, or the occasional drop of pool water dripped from his hair onto her taut back.

'What's wrong?'

'I'm a bit sore,' she lied. She damn well wasn't going to tell him just his mere touch had such a strong effect on her.

'Silly girl.' His voice was a velvet whisper. 'With skin like yours you shouldn't be out unprotected in the sun.'

The sun was the least of her worries at the moment! As his skilful hands massaged in the oil Tabitha had to remind herself to breathe. Her stomach knotted as they moved slowly across her shoulders. She could feel her nipples hardening, jutting into the sunbed like soldiers standing to attention; a pulse was flickering between her thighs, her blood running like mercury towards her groin. With one hand still on her back, he squeezed the bottle onto her left thigh and the oil, melting in the heat, ran like a river between her legs.

Almost faint with longing, she felt his hand touch her sun-kissed legs, his fingers working in small circular motions, moving higher, ever higher. Only a gentle snore from Marjory broke the oppressive silence, and Tabitha lay there, grinding her teeth together to hold back the groan in her throat.

Zavier might just as well have been massaging accelerant into her skin; one tiny spark and surely her body would explode in flames. It took a superhuman effort to lie there and for all the world appear detached, to pretend that it wasn't the man she loved massaging her so skilfully.

'That should keep the rays off.'

She felt the sunbed lift as he stood up, and she waited,

waited for the sensations overpowering her to abate, for the burning, aching longing he had initiated to subside. But it didn't.

She lay there another ten minutes or so, her eyes tightly shut, feigning sleep. But she knew Zavier wasn't fooled, that he was more than aware of the passion he had awoken.

'It's too warm for me,' Tabitha said finally, when she could take it no more. Standing, she grabbed at a towel, pulling it around her so he wouldn't see her swollen nipples, the arousal he had instigated. 'I'm going inside.'

'Why?' His voice was low but she could hear the mirth in it. 'Things are only just starting to hot up.'

Oh, the bliss of the icy cool water as she splashed her face then rested her face against the tiles. Tabitha fought the image of his hands on her body, the sheen of lust in his expressive eyes. How could one man have such a hold on her? How could one man turn her world around like this? Why did Zavier Chambers have this effect on her?

Because she loved him.

The answer was as simple as it was complicated. Lust, passion, power—they all played their part. But this was good old-fashioned love. She had loved him from the moment she had laid eyes on him in the church. She loved everything about him.

But Zavier Chambers despised her; he thought she was the worst kind of woman. The pain of that thought was enough to calm her twitching body, enough to temper the wild thoughts that were cascading through her mind.

Peeling off her bikini top, she fiddled with the shower control before catching her reflection in the mirror.

Tabitha gazed back at her own glittering eyes, searching for an answer to the impossible conundrum.

'You've only yourself to blame,' she said darkly to her image. 'You've only got yourself to blame for all this.'

'My thoughts exactly.'

Jumping with shock, she saw the dark brooding reflection of Zavier standing in the bathroom doorway.

'How long have you been there?' Her eyes were glittering now, with anger and embarrassment. 'How long have you been watching me?'

Zavier laughed, but there was no warmth in it. 'Don't worry—I don't need to get my kicks peering through a keyhole. Why would I?' He crossed the bathroom slowly and she shrank back against the sink. 'When we both know I can have you any time I want.'

'How dare you?'

'It's a bit late for false modesty.' He put a hand up to her burning cheek, running his finger along its length and down her neck, halting teasingly as he came to the soft naked mounds of her breasts. 'My, you have caught the sun, haven't you? Perhaps you should have let me oil your front.'

Angrily brushing past him, she fled for the safety of her room. But there was no haven to be found there: the bed seemed to mock her, forcing an instant recall of another place, another time, their tumbling bodies replaying in her mind like some erotic foreign movie stumbled upon by accident, their limbs locked in tremulous unison more erotic than any fantasy.

'Only business, huh?' He strode over to her, one finger flicking her nipple, giving a knowing, mocking smile as it swelled at the merest touch. His other hand was expertly untangling the tie of her bikini bottom. 'All just an act, huh?'

She should have run—slapped him, kicked him—but she stood there rigid, every muscle, every taut nerve shivering with shameful desire.

'I can have you any time I want,' he repeated.

He was poisonous, arrogant and loathsome; but he was right, damn him. He was so right, and there was nothing she could say otherwise.

'You want me, Tabitha.' He spat her name.

'I don't.' Her voice was a mere croak. He had freed one strap and now ran a teasing finger through the damp Titian mound of down as he plied the other strap, his breath hot and hard on her warm oiled body. The towel slinked around his hips slithered down without a sound, and she started in excitement at the angry swelling that baited her, that summoned her body just by its presence. 'I don't.'

She was naked now, exposed. He threw the saffron garment aside, parting her legs with his hand. He slid his fingers into her warmth as her throat constricted against a gasp of protest.

'I don't remember oiling you here.'

Her breathing matched his now, gasping, uneven, and she felt herself contract around his fingers, felt her body arching towards his.

'Tell me to stop and I will.' His thumb was massaging her swollen nub as his fingers snaked inside her slippery warmth. 'Tell me to stop,' he ordered, pushing her back onto the bed, parting her legs further with his muscular thigh.

His erection teased her at the entrance to her Nirvana, a tiny thrust that took her to the edge. She was pushing against him now, urging him to come deeper, but still he held back, the swell of him awaiting the formal invitation that she was loath yet desperate to give.

'Tell me to stop.'

She shook her head, Titian curls splaying over the pillows. 'No!'

'No, you don't want me, or no, don't stop?'

His restraint was agony, his manhood swelling at her entrance as her legs wrapped like a vice around him.

'No, don't stop,' she gasped.

Still he made her wait, inching his way just a fraction deeper as she writhed beneath him.

'Say you want me,' he ordered, and though it repulsed her to beg she was beyond reason, her need for him so urgent nothing else mattered.

'I want you!' She was nearly screaming, her legs coiling around him as he plunged into her, swelling the instant he entered her, their bodies exploding in unison, contracting, tightening as the world rushed around them. With a moan he collapsed on her, groaning, the last shuddering spasms of their union pulsing together as they lay in the moistened sheen of their skins. And as she lay there, listening to his breathing even out, one arm wrapped around her, the lazy hand softly cupping her bottom, his maleness filling the air she breathed, tears sprang from her eyes.

Surely she could tell him now? Surely, deep down, he must already know?

It took a second to register that the telephone was ringing, but her anger at the intrusion paled as she heard the thin, thready voice of her grandmother.

He watched her as she took the call, watched the rosy glow of her cheeks fade as she held the telephone, her knuckles white around the receiver, her lips taut as she mumbled into the phone.

'Was that your bookie?'

His attempt at a joke didn't even raise a smile, and with a start he watched the tears form in Tabitha's eyes, her lashes crushing the moisture as she screwed her eyes shut and fought for control.

'What's happened?' His voice was clipped, formal, even as he snapped into the businessman that he was: ready to deal at a second's notice with whatever was thrown at him.

'My grandmother,' Tabitha started, 'she's sold the house.'

'To pay off her debt?'

Tabitha shrugged; pulling the sheet around her, she covered her breasts. 'I'd already taken care of that.' She looked up. 'Or rather you had.' Her fingers were pleating the sheet; she was chewing her bottom lip as she dealt with the bombshell that had just exploded. 'She's sold up and is moving into a retirement village with a man she's apparently fallen head over heels in love with. She's going to pay me back—that was why she rang. She wanted to tell me before the wedding.'

'So you wouldn't have to go through with it?' His voice was strained, hoarse, his austere façade disintegrating with every word. 'Did you tell her our marriage was all a sham?'

'No.' Tears were streaming now, his apt description the salt in the wound. 'She thought it would make things easier for us—you know, a young couple starting out and all that...'

'We're hardly teenagers.'

'I told her that,' Tabitha agreed, wiping her cheeks with the edge of the sheet. 'And I told her she didn't have to rush—after all, we wouldn't exactly have starved.'

'What do you mean?'

'Well, it's not as if you need the money…'

'I meant why the sudden past tense, Tabitha? What's with the "we wouldn't have"? Shouldn't you be saying "we won't"?'

'I can pay you back the money I owe you,' she sobbed, looking at his perplexed face. 'She's sold her house, I tell you. His name's Bruce…'

'I don't give a damn what his name is.' Realisation was dawning for both of them, with aching clarity, and he ran a hand through his tousled hair, the muscle jumping in his cheek the only sign he was anything other than completely calm. 'I could still make you go through with it,' he hissed. 'The contract covered everything.'

Not quite. Tabitha fiddled with the stone on her finger. Not once did it mention love. She could feel the moisture of their lovemaking between her legs, slipping away from her as surely as Zavier was. 'You can't force me, Zavier, you've no hold over me now. I can back out if I want to.'

He stood up, walking over to the window and staring broodingly outside, his nakedness mocking her now, a teasing taste of what she could have had—for six months at least.

'But I won't.' His back was to her. She saw the set of his shoulders, the quilted muscles beneath the olive skin, and she ached to reach out for him. 'I still want to marry you.'

She watched him stiffen more, if that was possible.

'Why?'

Still his back was to her; still he couldn't bring himself to look at her. Tabitha was grateful for the reprieve. This was hard enough without being humiliated further, seeing the scorn, the triumph in his eyes when she told him she loved him.

'Because…' The words were there but her mouth simply wouldn't obey her. 'Isn't it obvious? Do I have to spell it out?'

He turned then. The scorn she had predicted was there in his eyes, but there wasn't even a trace of triumph, just a sneering look of distaste.

'Money?' His lips twisted around the word. 'God, you're even more desperate for it than I thought.'

She could have put him right then, pleaded her case and told him the truth, but what purpose would it have served? He was as damaged as Aiden; sure, he didn't drown himself in alcohol, but his problems ran just as deep, his soul was just as damaged. Not once had it even entered his head that her reason for sleeping with him, for agreeing to this charade, for marrying him, might be love.

'Do you know why I despise you so much, Tabitha?'

She didn't want to know, didn't want to hear his scathing comments, but some sadistic streak made her answer. Running a tongue over her dry lips, she heard her voice come out in a coarse whisper. 'Why?'

'Because beneath that smile, beneath that trusting little face and that easygoing laugh, you're as hard as nails.' He glanced at his watch. 'This time tomorrow you'll be Mrs Tabitha Chambers—if a bolt of lightning doesn't strike you down first.' Slamming out of the adjoining door into his own room, he left her there, on the bed, shocked and reeling at his outburst.

She ached to go after him, to somehow explain that money had nothing to do with this—but what was the point?

She felt sorry for him.

Sorry that his life had left him so scarred, so untrusting that he simply didn't believe in love.

Six months.

Six months of holding him at night, waking to him each morning. The mental abacus was starting again. One hundred and eighty days to shower love on him, to show him that life could be so much sweeter, so much easier with love on your side.

This time tomorrow she would be wearing his ring, would be blessed with the saving grace of time.

This time tomorrow she would tell him she loved him.

CHAPTER ELEVEN

'YOU look beautiful.'

Tabitha smiled at Aiden's reflection in the mirror as he slipped into the room.

'She'd look even better if she stayed still for five minutes,' Carla the hairdresser grumbled as she pierced Tabitha's scalp with yet another pin. Checking the tiara was firmly secured, she almost asphyxiated her client with yet another waft of hairspray before standing back to admire her handiwork. 'He's right; you do look beautiful.'

Even Tabitha agreed. The sophisticated woman staring demurely back at her from the mirror was nothing like the dizzy redhead she knew so well. The wild Titian curls were sleek and straight, caught at the back of her neck in an elegant chignon, her fringe was smooth and silken, falling seductively over one eye, and though she felt as if she were wearing a ton of make-up her complexion looked clear and smooth, with a dusting of rose on her cheeks and her eyeshadow a smudgy brown, accentuating the jade eyes. Only her lips were heavy, the dusky red tones making her mouth look wide and sensual.

'Thought this might help,' Aiden said once Carla had gone. Holding two glasses up, he pulled a bottle of champagne from under his jacket. 'I swiped it from one of the tables.' Expertly popping the cork, he handed her a glass before proposing a toast.

'To my dear friend Tabitha, who after today will also

be my sister-in-law. The sisterly advice will still be freely available, I hope?' he asked in a jokey voice after draining his glass in one.

'Of course.'

'And this is still all about business?' The jokey edge had gone, his voice cautious, his eyes concerned.

Tabitha hesitated, but only for a second. Confiding in Aiden was practically second nature, after all, but this was one thing Zavier definitely deserved to hear first. 'Absolutely.'

'You know, despite my earlier reservations, this wedding isn't turning out to be such a bad thing after all. My father's so delighted with the whole caboodle he seems to have forgotten to be angry with me. I took him for a walk this morning. We couldn't go on the beach, obviously, what with his chair, but I pushed him along the pier and we spoke.'

'How was it?'

Aiden shrugged. 'Better than it has been. He even made a few noises about going to look at my paintings. Apparently Zavier's been to see them and persuaded Dad to take a look.'

'Zavier went to see them?'

'Yep. He's a dark horse, isn't he? After the way he's criticised my painting, never in a million years did I think he'd actually be the one sticking up for me, and to Dad of all people. You just can't imagine how much that meant to me. Dad still managed a few barbs, though, about how I needed to face up to life, grow up and all that, but on the whole it was great.'

After putting on her dress, Tabitha lifted the sheer, simple veil as Aiden pulled up her zip. 'Maybe he's worried about your drinking,' she ventured nervously, slipping on her mules so she wouldn't have to look at him.

'Not you as well,' Aiden groaned. 'Darling, you're even starting to sound like an old married woman.'

'I care about you, Aiden, and…' Her voice trailed off. She was scared of pushing, yet scared to say nothing when it was so obviously needed.

'Go on,' Aiden offered, with a slight edge to his voice. 'Don't stop now.'

'You *do* drink too much.'

'Said the gambler to the alcoholic.'

Tabitha smiled. 'And *you're* starting to sound like your brother; he used the same line on me a while back.' Her hand touched his arm. It wasn't the time, it wasn't the place, but Aiden was her friend and some things just had to be said.

Perhaps it was a day for the truth.

'You're drinking every day, Aiden, and for the best part of it too. I'm allowed to be worried.'

'Not today you're not. Today you just have to worry about looking beautiful.' He stood back and stared at her slowly as she looked at her reflection in the full-length mirror.

'Which you do; if I didn't know otherwise I'd say you look every bit the blushing bride. You know, Tab, if I wasn't gay you'd be the woman of my dreams.'

She gave a small laugh. The simple lilac velvet dress hugged her curves, slipping over the hollows of her stomach. The gentle gathering at the bust accentuated her full soft breasts, the thin straps not detracting from her delicate collarbone where her one and only heirloom glittered—a diamond necklace her father had once given to her mother. She fingered the stone, overcome with sadness for what she had lost so young, for the family cruelly torn apart and for what her parents had lost: the dream of seeing their daughter walking down the aisle.

Aiden was right, she looked every bit the blushing bride, but despite the lies, despite the circumstances, the guilt was gone.

All of it.

When the music played, when she walked on Aiden's arm to join her future husband, she would be doing it with a clear conscience and with her parents' blessing; she just knew that deep down. As she spoke her vows her voice would be steady, for she would be speaking the truth.

Because she loved him.

'I got you this.' Digging in his pocket, Aiden pulled out a diamond bracelet. He had to hold her shaking hand steady as he clipped it on.

'It's beautiful. But, Aiden, I thought you said you weren't getting any presents.'

He shook his head. 'This isn't a wedding present; it's a friendship bracelet. Even when you're an old divorcee and moaning about Zavier we're still going to be best friends. Hey,' he said, alarmed as tears welled in her eyes. 'You'll ruin your make-up.'

'I'm sorry.' His crack about divorce hadn't exactly helped, but given the emotion of the moment Aiden let it pass without too much inspection and gently wiped a stray tear away. 'Thanks for doing this today, Aiden. I'm glad you're here with me.'

'I wouldn't be anywhere else.' Glancing at his watch, he offered his arm. 'Come on, you, let's get this over with. I'm dying for a Scotch.' A tiny wink creased his left eye as Tabitha's lips pursed. 'I know I need help, Tab, and I really am going to do something about it. I just need to get used to the idea for a while. A lifetime of abstinence doesn't really sound my forte.'

He stood there smiling and she took his arm, her dearest friend holding her as they walked through the house and across the lawn.

An arch of roses was the only barrier between Tabitha and her vows, and she listened as the orchestra paused and the congregation stilled.

'You're sure about this?' Aiden offered for the very last time.

Her heels were sinking in the grass, butterflies jumping in her stomach as she listened to the delicious sound of Wagner trickling through the hazy afternoon air. Stepping on to the carpet, she fiddled with her dress before taking Aiden's arm.

'I'm sure,' she said softly.

'Then let's go.'

Every eye turned as she stepped through the arch. She heard the gasps for a fleeting moment, saw the congregation—her friends, her grandmother with her partner, Marjory, grinning widely, Jeremy pale and proud beside her—and then her eyes were on Zavier.

He swallowed as she entered, his eyes meeting hers, his hands clenched by his sides as his chin jutted upwards. She knew he was nervous, and so was she, but her confidence in this unison, her utter love for him, was enough for them both.

They walked slowly, Aiden steadying her, beaming faces welcoming her as she walked to the man she loved.

And though in the days that followed Tabitha would rewind and replay the scene like a perpetual video in her mind, she would never be quite sure how it actually happened. Whether Marjory's piercing scream or the loud crash came first.

Her first ridiculous thought was that the bolt of lightning Zavier had darkly predicted had somehow come to fruition, but just as she discarded that notion, as she watched the gaze of the crowd frantically turn to the front, she registered that Jeremy was lying on the floor, his grey face darkening, blue around the lips, his body limp, spread-eagled where he had collapsed to the floor.

It was Tabitha who moved first. Everyone else stood frozen to the spot, the video stuck on freeze-frame. With her heart in her mouth Tabitha raced over. Already breathless from the emotion of seeing Zavier, she had to force herself to slow down, to calmly and methodically assess the situation and do what little she could.

'Jeremy!' She called his name loudly, once maybe twice, as her trembling hand reached for Jeremy's neck, her long fingers searching for a pulse. Her eyes moved to his chest, looking for a movement, the tiniest indication that he was breathing. She could feel every eye on her. An eerie silence had descended and there was no need to call for quiet as she placed an ear to the lifeless chest, listening for a heartbeat, listening for the breath of life, frantically trying to remember what she should do, to recall the information she had learnt on a long-ago first aid course.

'He's not breathing; I don't think his heart's beating.' Looking up, she surveyed the stunned and horrified crowd. She had wrongly expected some sort of reaction to her statement, for someone to snap to attention, for some assistance. But no one was moving.

No one except Zavier. Kneeling astride his father, after a momentary pause he took control in an instant. 'Someone call an ambulance—is anyone a doctor?'

Bending forward, he pinched his father's nose and gave him the kiss of life, nodding briefly as Tabitha leant on the lifeless, still chest and pushed as she had seen on the television, berating herself over and over for her lack of knowledge, for the awkward giggles expended in that first aid course when she really should have listened.

'Can I help?'

The oldest man Tabitha had ever seen was being pushed forward by a tearful Marjory, his old bones leaning heavily on a walking stick, small eyes magnified by the thickest glasses imaginable.

'Gilbert's the family doctor,' Marjory sobbed.

A smile that was absolutely out of place tugged at the corner of her lips as she registered Zavier's horror, and, most amazingly of all, when his eyes briefly met hers he returned her smile.

'We're doing fine,' Zavier clipped between breaths. 'Perhaps Gilbert could ring Melbourne, line up Dad's cardiac doctor.'

Her hair was plastered to her head with sweat, her arms aching with the sheer exertion of keeping Jeremy's heart pumping, and she knew she couldn't go on for much longer.

'Aiden, help me here.' She looked at the stricken face of her dearest friend and her heart went out to him, but she needed his help. 'Aiden?' she pleaded.

But all Aiden could do was stand and weep. 'Please, Dad, breathe,' he begged, tears streaming down his face as she worked on the inert body of his father.

'Do you want to swap?' Zavier offered, but Tabitha shook her head, knowing Zavier was working just as hard as her and that seconds lost in moving would be seconds Jeremy needed.

On she worked, the hot sun on the back of her neck,

her eyes blurry from sweat and make-up and mascara that clearly wasn't as waterproof as it said on the tube, almost weeping with relief when finally the sound of sirens in the distance permeated the sultry afternoon air.

Exhausted, she leant back on her heels as the paramedics took over, clipping endless monitors to the still lifeless body, pushing oxygen into his mouth through a bag. Tabitha tried to move back on cramped legs that wouldn't obey her.

'We're going to shock him,' the paramedic said sombrely, and Tabitha knew that it was now or never. 'Everybody back.'

Strong arms lifted her out of the way, and without looking she knew instinctively it was Zavier.

The defibrillator paddles were placed on Jeremy's chest and they all stood back as the paramedic delivered an electric shock in an attempt to restore the chaotic rhythm of Jeremy's heartbeat.

'Again. Everybody back.'

Her legs were trembling so violently she thought she might sink back to the floor. But Zavier's strong arms were still around her, holding her tightly as they stared transfixed at the monitor. Her mind was on Jeremy, willing him to live, and yet with Zavier's arms around her she couldn't help but draw from his strength, couldn't help but lean on him slightly. Never had she felt closer to him.

Surely now there must be a chance for them?

A loud blip emanated from the monitor, and they watched as the flat green line flickered once, then twice, and then again, the blips becoming more frequent. An audible sigh of relief filled the room as Jeremy's heart reverted to a stable rhythm.

'Thank God,' Tabitha muttered, more to herself than

anyone else, but for some reason her words seemed to incense Zavier. As if suddenly conscious that he was touching her, holding her, he dropped her out of his arms as if he was holding hot coal.

'Why the relief?' he snapped, his eyes full of hatred, contempt. 'Were you worried you mightn't get the second instalment?'

With horror, Tabitha swung to face him, her optimism of a moment before, the slim belief that now there might be a chance for them, evaporating in the heat that radiated from his eyes. But there was no time to argue the point. Jeremy Chambers had to take precedence here.

This was no time to tell him she loved him.

'Is there anything else I can do?' Ashen, trembling, she offered her assistance to the paramedics as Zavier organised the guests to clear chairs and prepare a makeshift landing pad.

'The best thing you can do is to have a large brandy, love. Not the nicest thing to happen at your wedding, is it? We're waiting for the helicopter to arrive. We're going to take him direct to Melbourne.'

Aiden, shouting into a mobile phone, came over then. 'The doctors are on standby.'

'I'm coming with him.' Marjory's affected tearful tones carried across the garden.

'Sorry, love.' The paramedic shook his head. 'He's really too sick.'

'I'm coming,' Marjory said resolutely, her voice void of hysteria now. There was an air of authority and a strange dignity as she knelt beside the stretcher and took Jeremy's lifeless hand. Turning briefly, she looked the paramedic square in the eye. 'I won't get in the way; you have my word. If my husband is about to die I want to be with him.'

'I'll look after her.' Aiden was grey himself, trembling violently, his teeth chattering noisily. 'She ought to be with him.'

The whirring chopper blades heralded the arrival of the transfer team. Everyone was moved back as it landed, its whirring blades buffeting the marquee, ladies' hats and dresses flapping as the noise drowned out any conversation.

As they loaded Jeremy into the back Aiden turned to Tabitha, squeezing her hands tightly. 'I'll see you at the hospital.'

But Zavier had other ideas. 'You'll do no such thing. I'm taking her back to her house and then *I'll* meet you at the hospital.'

'But she ought to be there,' Aiden argued.

'What for?' he snapped. 'We both know she's not the caring daughter-in-law to be. Mum and Dad are the only concern here. Look after them and I'll meet you there just as soon as I can.'

The paramedics were ready to go now, and there was no time to debate the issue.

'Keep your chin up, Aiden.' Tabitha kissed him fondly on his tear-streaked cheek. 'Everything will work out.'

If only she could believe her own words.

He stood over her as she packed, not saying a word, his dark eyes watching her every move as Tabitha piled her possessions into her suitcase.

'Could you leave me alone for just five minutes?'

She desperately needed to go to the bathroom, to peel off her dress, undo her hair, to somehow remove every trace of the awful charade she had engineered. Dressed in her best, she seemed to embody the hard-faced bitch

Zavier assumed she was, and suddenly it seemed imperative he saw her as she was, not as the sleek, sophisticated woman of earlier.

'I'm not going anywhere. Just hurry up, will you?'

'Are you scared that I might run off with a few choice items?'

'It did enter my head.'

His patience snapped then. It was almost as if he couldn't bear to watch her a moment longer; couldn't stand being in the same room any longer than absolutely necessary. Pulling out the top drawer of the dresser, he tipped the contents into her case. She watched with mounting trepidation as he strode over to the wardrobe, grabbing her dresses and piling them into the case without even bothering to take them off their hangers.

Her underwear drawer was the next recipient of his simmering anger. Grabbing handfuls of lingerie, his face livid with unvented rage, he tossed them on top of her dresses before snapping the case firmly closed.

'Anything that's been left behind I'll have sent on to you. Now come on.'

'Please, Zavier, can I just come to the hospital? Surely your mother will expect me to be there?'

'My God, you just don't give up, do you? It's over, Tabitha. The wedding is off—we don't have to pretend any more.'

'I didn't mean for that. I just want to see how Jeremy is—how you all are…' The thought of going home without knowing if Jeremy had lived or died was unbearable, but more to the point she wanted to be there for Zavier, to help him through what would undoubtedly be the worst night of his life.

Because that was what lovers did: they were there for each other.

But Zavier had other ideas. 'Save the crocodile tears; I'm taking you home, Tabitha.'

He didn't even wait for her to put on her seat belt, accelerating out of the drive as if the devil himself were chasing them. She sat there shivering and stunned, staring out of the side window, watching the dark inky ocean whizzing past as his car hugged the bay road.

The drive to Lorne had taken hours, probably because she had wanted to get there. But now she didn't want to leave suddenly time seemed to be moving faster, the shimmering night skyline of Melbourne drawing ever nearer. She dreaded arriving. However strained the silence, however huge the loathing emanating from him, any contact, however painful, was better than none. The bleak empty wilderness of her life stretched before her: a life without Zavier.

This had never been part of the game, had never been the intended prize; love had come when everyone had said it would: when she was least expecting it.

And losing it for ever hurt like hell.

He pulled over into a lookout, a move that surprised Tabitha, who sat staring ahead as he opened the door and without a word left the car. Idly staring into the night sky, his profile strong in the moonlight, he stood motionless.

Unsure, she sat a moment in the car, memorising every last detail of him. As if sensing her longing, he turned his head, raising his hand to beckon her to join him.

'It's all right.' His lips hardly moved as he spoke. 'I'm not about to throw you in.'

She managed a shallow laugh as she teetered towards him, her high heels no match for the sandy inlet. 'Thank goodness. I'd sink like a stone with all the cutlery I shoved down my bra.'

The tiny spark of humour between them shifted the mood away from the volatile anger of before; he looked sad now—jaded, perhaps, but infinitely more approachable.

'Shouldn't you be getting to the hospital?' she ventured.

'I don't want to go,' he replied simply.

Honestly.

She didn't know how to respond; hearing the break in his voice tore at her heart.

'I just need a moment; it's going to be pretty messy when I get there.' He swallowed hard and she realised then the pain he was in. How hard it must be for Zavier at times like this. How hard it must be to always be the strong one, to have everyone leaning on you, turning to you for every last thing. The lynchpin of the family, the breadwinner, the organiser, and sometimes the adjudicator.

'He might make it.' She tried to inject some hope into her voice, tried to give him something to cling to, something to sustain him, but miracles seemed in short supply today.

Zavier shrugged helplessly. 'It doesn't look great, though, does it? I know that really there's no chance, that this surely must be it. Tabitha, what I said to you about the contract—I really didn't mean it. I'm truly sorry for my words. You were amazing back there, and if my father does live he owes his life to you.'

Tabitha knew then that this was her only chance. If she didn't say it now, couldn't be there for him, to support him through what was undoubtedly about to come, then there wasn't much point.

Maybe Zavier was right, maybe her grandmother's affliction was hereditary, for she was about to take the biggest gamble of her life.

'I didn't do it for money.' The words were out now, and she swallowed, watching closely for his reaction.

'I know, and I had no right to imply that you did. I just saw red all of a sudden. I thought he was dead...'

'I'm not talking about your father's heart attack.' Her teeth were chattering as badly as Aiden's had been, but she forced herself to take a deep breath and calm down. 'I love you, Zavier. I always have. I wasn't marrying you for money.'

She heard the hiss of his breath as he exhaled loudly, stepped back as she watched his face darken, jumped as she heard the venom of his attack. 'My God, I wondered how long it would take you to play your last card.'

She'd never expected him to take her in his arms, to accept her words without question, but the pungent delivery of his statement was a million miles away from any scenario she had tentatively imagined.

'What do you mean?' Her arms shot out to him, as if somehow by touching him she might reach him, might make him hear the truth in her words. 'I love you, Zavier. I honestly love you.'

'Please.' He flicked her hand away, cruelly, dismissively. 'Have you any idea how many women have said that to me? "Oh, Zavier, this has nothing to do with money."' His voice simpered in a derisive generalisation of the female population, then returned to its harsh reality. 'This has everything to do with money, Tabitha. That was all it was ever about. And do you know what the saddest part is—the saddest bloody part of this whole charade?' He was shouting now, and she shook her head dumbly, shocked and stunned at the anger her declaration had unleashed. 'Believe it or not, I actually loved you.'

He stopped then, as stunned as she was by the admission.

It was Tabitha who broke the silence. 'You love me?' she gasped, her voice choked with wonder. But he broke in quickly, shattering her one second of salvation.

'Loved you,' he corrected. 'Past tense, Tabitha. That's all you'll ever be to me. I've spent my whole life wondering how my father could have been so weak, how he could have stayed with my mother knowing that she didn't love him, knowing she was only there for the life he could give her.' Finally his eyes found hers. 'And then you came along, Tabitha…'

She stood there transfixed, listening with tears streaming down her face to his revelations.

'And suddenly I didn't think my father was so weak any more. I actually understood him. That first night we met, my intention was to get you to my room—a kiss, perhaps, just enough to prove what I already knew—that you didn't love Aiden—to shame you into staying away from him. It was never my intention to…' He closed his eyes fleetingly. 'I don't think I need to remind you what happened, but in case you missed it I fell in love that night—fell so hard it hurt. I spent the next five days trying to work out how I could see you again, how to be with you, how to stop you taking up Aiden's offer of marriage.'

'I was never going to accept it,' she pleaded, but it fell on deaf ears.

'I could have married you knowing it was a business deal. I even figured that once you'd had a taste of the high life you might hang around—we could even have made it to forty years, like my parents. Yesterday, when you told me it wasn't your debt, I felt sick, physically sick at the prospect of losing you. I felt like the biggest heel in the world for still making you stick to the contract, but it was nothing compared to the terror I felt when you realised you could pay me back. I didn't want to lose you, Tabitha.'

'You don't have to,' she argued, tears coursing down her cheeks, begging for him to listen, to finally understand. But her tears didn't move him, didn't sway him an inch from the lonely moral high ground he was taking.

'I could almost have lived with it. Knowing you were with me for the lifestyle didn't seem to matter so long as I had you in my arms at night. But I knew the one thing I wouldn't be able to bear was you pretending that you loved me; the one thing I wouldn't be able to stand was hearing you lie to me.'

'I'm not lying now, Zavier. You have to believe me…'

'You're a con-artist, Tabitha.' The venom returned to his voice then, his words ripping at her very core. 'You've beguiled each and every one of us at every turn. First you're Aiden's girlfriend, then a gambler, then you change your story when it suits you so your grandmother's the one with the problem—and then, when it all falls through, when there's no chance I'll marry you, you throw in the fact you supposedly love me in an attempt to win me round.'

'But I do love you,' she pleaded. 'I have since that first night…'

'I might be weak where you're concerned but I'm not a fool. How can I ever believe a word that you say?'

The full magnitude of her loss hit her then—a loss of insurmountable proportions. This sophisticated, strong, beautiful man had loved her. This aching, gaping void, which would surely be her life now, was the price of her deception.

What had started as a silly game had cost her dearly.

There was no point arguing over the small details, no point pleading her case; she was guilty as charged, and though the sentence was harsh there was nothing to gain from an appeal.

Just the hell of agony prolonged.

The tears that had started at the outlook flowed unchecked as they drove on, the ocean too quickly replaced by the freeway, the city drawing closer and closer and closer, until finally it was upon them. The car slowed down as it drove through the empty late-night streets. Every light was green, of course, as if the whole world was conspiring to ensure the imminent ending was a swift one.

Popping the boot, he stayed in the front, clenching the steering wheel as she hauled her suitcase onto the street and up the path, her heels clipping noisily as she dragged the case along. But he didn't drive off; she had known he wouldn't. Ever the gentleman, despite his wrath, he would see her safely inside.

It only took a second of rummaging through her bag for her to realise that her keys weren't where they should be.

So much for a dignified exit!

Of all the times to misplace the blessed things, this wasn't the one Tabitha would have chosen. Looking up, she saw the irritated set of his chin, his fingers drumming impatiently on the steering wheel. She could almost hear the pained sigh as he threw open the car door and stepped out.

'What now?'

'It doesn't matter.' She tossed her head defiantly. 'You go on to the hospital.'

'I would if you'd just get inside.'

'I've lost my keys.'

The roll of his eyes was too much for her already strained nerves. 'Well, if you hadn't rushed me...' she argued.

'Sorry about that.' His face was white in the street-light, his lips set in a thin line as he strode over. 'I just wasn't banking on my father suffering a cardiac arrest and then having to police my fiancée from rushing off with the family silver. Next time I'll be more patient.'

His biting sarcasm actually helped! Enough anyway to dry up her tears and return the fire to her eyes.

'There's a small window round the back. If I break it I can get my hand in and undo the laundry door lock.'

Without a word he turned on his heel, walking smartly along the side of the house, not even bothering to part the rather overgrown fauna that she'd never quite got around to trimming.

'I can manage,' she said proudly.

'Sure, and were you planning to smash the glass with your bare hand?'

She hadn't thought of that! 'I'm sure there's a towel or something in my case...'

He didn't even deign to give a response. Pulling off his jacket, he wrapped it around his arm and punched the glass out in one quick motion. Slipping his hand through, he promptly undid the lock.

'Not the safest property, is it?' he said dryly as she tiptoed her way through the glass. 'You should see about getting someone in to put some security screens up.'

'Save it, Zavier. My safety's not your concern; you've made that abundantly clear.'

As she stepped into the laundry she lost her footing for a second in the darkness. His hand shot out to save her in a reflex action, steadying her from falling, perhaps, but sending her body into absolute overdrive.

The world stopped for a moment; his skin seemed to sear her flesh. Tabitha half expected to look down and see blisters forming around the strong grip of his fingers. Dragging her eyes up, she held his gaze. His contumelious words, the inscrutable features, couldn't mask the pain in his eyes or the passion that burnt there: a lexicon of the love she would now never know.

'I have to go.'

'I know.' With a sob she pulled the ruby off her finger. 'Here, you'd better take this.'

'Keep it.'

'I don't want it. You said it had to stay in the family...' She stood stricken as he took the ring, her words tailing off as he tossed it out of the broken window.

'What the hell do you think I'd need it for now?'

Stunned and reeling, she stood in the darkness of her laundry, listening to his footsteps echoing down the path, the slam of the car door, the deep purr of the engine as he pulled off into the darkness. And finally when there was nothing left of him to hear, when the draught from the open door had taken away every last trace of his powerful cologne, when the skin on her arm had stopped tingling from his touch, Tabitha flicked on the light. The shattered glass littering the floor, the jagged remains of what had once been her window, were so achingly akin to the remnants of her own life she might just as well be looking into a mirror.

CHAPTER TWELVE

Six months. That was all she had wanted.

Six months to show him how good and wonderful love could be, if only you'd let it.

Wandering home from work in her smart little boxy suit, she thought no one could have guessed the agony in each step, the burden of lugging around a broken heart.

Milk.

The most basic of daily chores took a huge mental effort these days.

Even the local milk bar was agony. Everything seemed to remind her of Zavier, from the mineral water to the daily papers headlining the amazing progress of Jeremy Chambers. How he had been wheeled into Emergency barely conscious, with an unrecordable blood pressure and a grim diagnosis. His appalling chances of survival were the only reason the surgeons had agreed to operate.

After all, you can't kill a dead man.

Amy Dellier even managed to flash a smile from the pages of the glossies, strategically placed at the check-out. It was as if in the short time she had known him Zavier had permeated every facet of her life, taken over every last one of her senses.

Arriving home, she was reminded of him sitting in the driveway as she scrabbled for her keys, and such was her longing she half expected to look up and see him sitting there in the car. As she opened her front door for a moment she was almost sure she could smell him.

Flicking listlessly through her mail, she felt her heart skip a beat as his flashy writing jumped out at her. Her hands shaking, she ripped open the envelope. She ignored the cheque that fell out as she hastily opened the letter inside. It didn't take long to read it—after all, it was only three little words.

> *As agreed*
> *Zavier.*

Just not the three little words she needed to hear.

Sure, Tabitha thought about putting on make-up, combing her hair and dressing up for the occasion. But she knew there wasn't any point. Why dress up for your own funeral?

Lining up at the bank, she watched the teller's eyebrows shoot up a fraction as she gave her withdrawal slip and without a word handed over her driver's licence to verify her signature.

'We normally require some notice when it's such a large withdrawal. We don't always have enough cash on the premises.'

Tabitha wasn't in the mood for games, or lectures. 'Can I have my money now? Yes or no?'

'It might take a few moments. Will you be happy to wait?'

She let out a low laugh. 'I'll wait, but I can't guarantee to be happy.'

A storm was breaking as she reached the high-rise office of Chambers Financiers. There must have been something in her stance, or perhaps it was the determination in her eyes, but even Zavier's receptionist let her past without much argument.

So what if she didn't have an appointment?

Zavier didn't stand as she entered, he didn't even look particularly surprised to see her—just gestured to the chair at his desk, watching as she sat down in a skirt that was too short and a jacket that was too big.

His office was huge. Her entire home could have been dropped in the middle and still left room for a courtyard. But then this was Chambers territory she was stepping into—why would she expect less?

'What can I do for you?' She felt like one of his clients for all the tenderness in his greeting. Even Zavier seemed to flinch at his own formality. 'I'm sorry, how have you been?'

'Fine,' she lied. 'Work's been busy.'

A hint of a frown marred his smooth face. 'Just finished a matinée?'

Tabitha shook her head. 'I've got a job in the box office. It looks a bit more respectable on an application form.'

Still the frown remained.

'What?' she ventured, blushing under his scrutiny.

'You just look…different, that's all.'

'Shackled' was the first word that sprang to his mind, but of course he didn't say it. Her red hair was pulled back, that gorgeous body draped in sombre navy, even the jade of her eyes seemed to have dimmed—but what Tabitha wore, what Tabitha did, for that matter, was her business and hers alone. Still, it was only polite to ask how she was doing…

'How come you're not dancing? If you're having any trouble getting a part because of taking a break, I could have a word—make a few noises.'

'You mean you'll take care of it?'

Zavier shifted uncomfortably in his seat. 'Something like that. Look, I don't want what happened between us to ruin your career.'

Tabitha let out a low laugh. 'It was hardly a career, as you so delicately pointed out on more than a few occasions. Anyway, it doesn't matter now. I'm hoping to start my own dance school some time next year; the office work will help.'

'How?' He gave a derisive laugh. 'It's a box office, Tabitha, hardly rocket science.'

'And you're still a pompous know-it-all.' That stopped him in his tracks long enough for Tabitha to open her bag and catch her breath. 'This came in the post.' She pushed the cheque towards him, remembering with a strange surge of power him doing the same.

Like her, he didn't even deign to give it a glance. 'That's right. It's what's due to you. There should have been a covering letter enclosed. You didn't break the contract, I did, so you're still entitled to the money.'

'I don't want it.'

He waved a dismissive hand and turned back to his computer. 'Up to you.'

Trembling, she stood up and, opening her bag, took out a wad of money and placed it in front of him.

'What's this?'

'What does it look like? You're the financial whizz; I thought at least you'd recognise money when you see it.'

'But what's it for?'

'The first payment you gave to me—it's all there.' She turned to go but he called her back.

'You don't have to do this, Tabitha. How can you afford it?'

'My grandmother paid me back, remember?'

'But what about your dance school?'

'It will happen,' she said assuredly. 'Perhaps not as quickly as I'd like, but it will definitely happen.' Her hand was on the door and she wrenched it open.

'Why didn't you just write a cheque?'

For a second she stiffened, then slowly she turned. Her wary eyes had a strange dignity about them. 'So you could humiliate me further by not cashing it?'

She stared at him for the longest time, trying to somehow entrench his features on her memory, to capture the indigo of his eyes, the beauty of his face, scanning them, filing them, storing them. Saving them up for the dreams she was destined to live on.

'Why the acrimony, Tabitha? We both knew what we were getting into.'

'Maybe you did, Zavier,' she said softly. 'It seems I was naive enough for both of us.'

And then it was over. All she had to do was close the door and he was out of her life for good. The worst part of it was that he didn't even call her back.

She hadn't really expected him to.

'Tabitha?' Aiden met her as he came out of the lift. He was dripping wet, his hair for once out of place. 'What are you doing here?'

'Tying up a few loose ends.' She forced a smile, forced a normal voice. 'I read that your dad's off the ventilator; that's good news.'

'Better than that—they moved him out of ICU today. The cardiac surgeons are still shaking their heads in disbelief that Dad actually survived the surgery.' Taking her elbow, he steered her nearer the wall, away from the traffic of people in the corridor. 'Dad knew all along about me, Tabitha; about me being gay, I mean.'

'He knew?' Even in her emotionally drained state, Tabitha still felt a surge of interest and shock.

'Yep. When the nurses were prepping him for Theatre he called me in; I guess he thought it was going to be a deathbed talk. All that stuff about wanting me to grow up—well, he actually meant to stop living a lie, to face the truth.'

'And did your mum know?'

'Yep.' He gave a low laugh. 'Apparently she knew all along; she just didn't want to upset my father in case he couldn't cope with it. She's fine with it. At least now it's all out in the open, and apparently it's even quite fashionable these days to have a gay son. It gives her something new to talk about at the tennis club. I'm officially out of the closet now. We should have a party to celebrate.'

When she didn't respond he looked at her sadly.

'Poor Tab. I feel so guilty.'

'Why...?'

'Because for everyone else things have worked out. My father's got a few years left in him, my secret's happily out of the closet and no one seems to mind, but as for you, darling Tabitha—well, you're the one who got hurt. You do love Zavier, don't you?'

The tears came then, fast and furious, big sobs that racked at her body. And Aiden stood there, his arm around her shoulder, offering her a handkerchief as she fought for control.

'I'm sorry.'

'It's me that should be sorry—sorry for all that I've put you through. It was me that started the whole thing.' He gave her a long hug. 'Oh, Tab, I did try to warn you. I told you he'd only...'

'Crush me in the palm of his hand.' She finished the

sentence for him. 'It's a pretty accurate description of how I'm feeling.'

'You'll get over him,' Aiden assured her. 'You always do...'

'Not this time.' She blew her nose noisily.

'I did try to talk to him, to tell him what a wonderful woman you are, but he just wasn't interested. Maybe I could have another go...'

'No.' She shook her head firmly. 'He's not interested in excuses. He still insists it was all about money.'

'Which is so bloody like him,' Aiden replied. 'You were doomed, darling, the day you cashed the cheque. My dear brother believes the rest of us should be as infallible and as honest as he is.'

'I can see where he's coming from,' Tabitha said defensively. 'You can hardly blame him for being suspicious of love, given the examples he's been set. I don't exactly come out of this as a paragon of virtue.' She blew her nose again. 'Anyway, it doesn't matter. It's over now.'

'We're still friends? I've been terrified to come over in case you throw a saucepan at me or something.'

She gave a strangled laugh, but it changed midway and she cried instead. 'Of course we're still friends; it's just different, that's all. I can't see you for a while, Aiden. I can't look at you and not think about him. Do you understand?'

He nodded sadly. 'I'll miss you.'

'I know. Look, I've really got to go. I'll call you in a few weeks, a few months—whatever it takes.'

'Please, Tab, wait. I'll have a driver take you home. It's started to storm outside—at least let me do that for you.'

She shook her head. 'I'd really rather walk.'

'But it's pouring.'

'Good, then no one will see me crying.'

He saw her into the lift, stood watching as the numbers carried her down before heading into Zavier's office.

I told you so.

For Aiden there was no pleasure in being proved right. None.

For a little while there he'd actually thought they might make it. His face darkening, he went into the office. Seeing Zavier sitting there, working at his desk for all the world acting as if nothing had happened, only angered him further.

Maybe he wasn't acting, Aiden figured.

Maybe Zavier really didn't care.

'I just saw Tabitha leaving in tears.' Aiden flicked on the television on the far side of Zavier's office, changing the channel from the stock market show Zavier preferred to one of the commercial channels.

Zavier didn't bother to look up, frowning at the noise from the television. 'She just paid me back; it must have hurt.' He expected a laugh, but when it didn't come he finally looked up, watching as Aiden shook the rain off his jacket before carefully hanging it up on the hook. 'Mind you, I'll never work her out. What did she agree to do it for if she was intending to pay me back?'

'You're such a bloody fool sometimes.'

Zavier's eyes narrowed. Aiden, who never got angry, who was always laughing, always joking, suddenly looked as if he might actually hit him. 'What the hell's your problem?'

'I'm gay!' Aiden shouted.

'So what's that got to do with it?'

'I'm gay,' Aiden repeated. 'Yet even I managed to work it out.'

Zavier stared at his brother, utterly perplexed as Aiden waved his hands dramatically in the air.

'What do you think Tabitha did it for? She loves you, you idiot. Though God knows why.'

'It was business,' Zavier said darkly. 'She did it for the money.'

'If that's the case what's this doing here?' Aiden gestured to the notes on the desk. 'And why was she crying in the hall, with unkempt hair and not a scrap of make-up.'

'Her hair's always unkempt.'

'No, it isn't—at least not in that way—and Tabitha *always* wears make-up. Always. I notice these things.'

'Because you're gay?' Zavier asked, his voice bewildered.

Aiden rolled his eyes. 'Because I'm not blind.'

'So what you're telling me,' Zavier said slowly, standing up and walking the long length of his office before finishing his sentence, shaking his head as he did so, 'is that she loves me? Tabitha really loves me?'

'Finally.' Aiden rolled his eyes and lowered himself into one of the sumptuous leather lounges, his calm demeanour exacerbating Zavier's nervous pacing.

'So what should I do?'

'That I can't help you with. But I think it would be much better if you go to her now.'

'Because she's upset?' He was stalling, confused and unsure, wanting so much to believe what he was hearing, yet scared all the same.

'Maybe.' Aiden shrugged, pouring himself a large Scotch. 'But, more to the point, my favourite soap starts in five and I want to concentrate.'

* * *

Listlessly she walked up the garden path. Her clothes were drenched, clinging to her body, and her hair dripped in coiled tendrils down her back, but she didn't care. Sure, she wasn't so pessimistic as not to realise this torturous melancholy would abate somewhat, given time, but Tabitha also knew that for as long as there was a breath still in her body she would love him.

The love she felt might rest for a while, might even fade to bearable proportions, but it would never relent.

The sun peeking out from behind a cloud did nothing to cheer her. What was the point of a silver lining when Zavier was gone? A bright glint in the grass caught her eye and with a start she realised it was the ring. Bending, she retrieved it, her eyes filling as she rubbed the soil from it. Painful memories were all she had now.

'Tabitha.'

She froze, the sound of his voice so utterly unexpected, she literally froze—which, Tabitha realised quickly, wasn't the best look when one was half bent over.

'Zavier.' She straightened up, taking the opportunity to force a calming breath into her burning lungs. 'I'm just off to the pawn shop. What do you reckon I'll get?'

'Tabitha, don't.'

She sniffed, wiping her nose with the back of her hand. Not the most elegant of moves, but she was past caring. 'Of course it probably needs a good clean, but I'm sure I'll get a few thousand. I've been digging for days trying to find it.'

'Tabitha, can you stop talking for a moment and look at me?'

'Why?' she asked rudely.

'Just look at me, please.'

She couldn't—couldn't do that without breaking down. So instead she focused somewhere over his shoulder.

'I know that you love me.'

She didn't respond.

'I know that I love you.'

Still she didn't move.

'Aren't you going to say anything?'

'What is there to say? I told you I loved you when your father had his heart attack. You told me that you loved me too then—oh, sorry, *had* loved me. But it didn't stop you walking away.'

'I was scared.'

Slowly, achingly slowly, she lifted her eyes to him.

'But why? How could you be scared of me when you're so powerful...?'

He put a finger to her lips, first to hush her but then the feel of her flesh under the nub of his index finger couldn't pass without recognition. Tracing the outline of her mouth, he gazed at her, his eyes shining with wonder and love.

'Tabitha, work doesn't scare me—that's why I'm good at it. I can look at a pile of figures and reports, scan a spreadsheet in ten seconds flat, and know instinctively what's right. And do you know why I find it easy?'

She shook her head, her curls moving as she did so, tinctured every shade of red as the emerging rays of the afternoon sun lit up her features.

'It's easy because it doesn't matter—not to me, anyway. That's why I'm so good at it. I can totally detach myself. I make a million or I lose a million; at the end of the day it's only money. But love...' He gave a low laugh, but there was a break in it. 'You can read all the signs, think you've got it right, that this is the one—but what if you're wrong? What then? I don't give a damn about money, Tab, but getting it wrong, losing my heart, being hurt, being used—I couldn't bear it. My head and my heart were telling me two different things.'

She knew there was more, knew that he hadn't finished talking. Suddenly they were back on the beach, gazing at the rising sun, taking a moment to regroup, lost in their own pregnant pause.

'I had my life worked out, had everything sorted. I knew exactly what I wanted and a marriage like my parents' wasn't on the agenda. And then you came along, Tabitha, a fiery redhead with an attitude to match, rewriting my rule book as you went along. I almost convinced myself I was trying to protect Aiden and my family when the truth is the only person I was trying to protect was me.'

'Protect from what?' She needed to hear it, to be absolutely sure that she wasn't imagining things, wasn't getting ahead of herself and reading far too much into his words. She closed her eyes as she awaited his response.

'From falling in love with you.' He kissed her then— his lips finding hers easily, their mouths moving in heated unison, the need to seal his words transcending all else. And when, breathless, she pulled away, when the need to finally explain, to justify her actions overcame her ardour, he held her as she spoke, soothing her as he might a child reliving a nightmare.

'I didn't do it for the money—or maybe I did. I sort of convinced myself that was why I was doing it.' Her words were as jumbled as her thoughts. 'I think I knew I loved you right from the start. Aiden certainly did. But

I knew it was impossible, that love wasn't part of the deal. I tried to tell you about the gambling…'

'I knew.' His words stopped the tirade of her confession. 'I knew way before you told me that you didn't have a problem; I just didn't want to hear it.' It was Zavier who was trembling now, Zavier laying it all on the line with everything to lose, Zavier searching her eyes for a reaction. 'For a gambling addict you've got an amazingly good credit rating.'

'You checked up on me?' Her lips were white now, her mind whirring as she relived the past weeks under this entirely different slant.

He nodded slowly; it was way too late for lies now.

'So you knew all along?' His admission had truly shocked Tabitha. Just when she'd thought he couldn't surprise her, that there was nothing left to reveal, again he had floored her. 'That night in the casino…' Her eyes darted down, then back to his, needing, demanding answers.

'My suspicions were confirmed then. You didn't even know how to take your free spin, Tabitha,' he pointed out. 'It was almost funny.…'

Almost.

'But you were so angry on the beach when I told you—furious…'

'Because I didn't want you to say it,' he explained, his only defence the love that blazed from his eyes. 'I didn't want it to be over before we'd even started, and I knew that once you'd told me the truth the only decent thing I could do was offer you a chance to get out.'

'But you didn't?'

'I couldn't.'

The raw honesty of his answer moved her, and the bemusement faded from her eyes.

'Can't you see, Tabitha, I couldn't risk losing you? I was just trying to buy some time.'

'Time's what we've wasted,' Tabitha said gently, her anger evaporating as she gazed at the man she adored, finally allowing the enormity of his love to softly wrap around her, to soothe and comfort her broken, aching heart. 'What are you doing?' She giggled through her tears as he knelt down in the mud swamp that was her garden. 'The neighbours will see.'

'Good.' He laughed, enjoying the sound of her laughter, her girlish embarrassment. The sparkle was back in her eyes now. 'You're not the only one who enjoys an audience, you know. This time we're going to do things the right way.' His voice was suddenly serious, love blazing from his eyes as he knelt before her and with shaking hands offered her the ring—*her* ruby ring. 'Tabitha Reece, will you marry me?'

Tabitha took the ring and slipped it on her finger, back to where it belonged, to where it always would be.

'Say something,' he urged.

'Why? I've already said yes to you,' Tabitha pointed out. 'Six weeks, two days and fifteen hours ago.'

'But that was only temporary,' Zavier said, doubt, angst creeping into his voice.

'No, Zavier,' Tabitha said softly. 'When I said yes I meant it. It was always for ever.'

EPILOGUE

'IT's embarrassing,' Aiden insisted, bouncing baby Darcy on his knee. 'Isn't it, sweetheart? Seeing your nanny and grandad carrying on like a couple of teenagers at your christening?' He peered more closely at his nephew's face. 'Tab, why's he going all red? Purple now—and what's that terrible smell?'

Grinning, Tabitha relieved him of her son. 'Well, I think it's lovely. It might have taken forty years and a heart attack, but seeing Marjory and Jeremy so devoted to each other is a real tonic. There's nothing embarrassing about it. Anyway, if you don't want to be late for your date you'd better push off. I'm going to change Darcy. Thanks for his wonderful present, Aiden, you shouldn't have.'

'Of course I should have, and tell him to hang on to it. That painting will be worth a fortune in a few years. Actually, Zavier—' Aiden lowered his voice '—I was hoping for a word before I go.'

Zavier rolled his eyes. 'How much this time?'

'It's all right for you,' Aiden said defensively. 'Dad's going to live for ever, at this rate, and maybe my paintings are taking off, but compared to you it's peanuts. Anyway, Luigi's got expensive tastes—I can hardly take him to the local burger bar. Have you seen the price of champagne these days?'

'You're supposed to be on the wagon,' Zavier said sharply.

'I am, but that doesn't mean Luigi has to be.'

'If he cares about you,' Zavier started, in a voice that could only denote a lecture, 'he won't mind where you take him. And stop rolling your eyes, you two. I'm right on this.'

'I hardly think a man who had to buy his bride should be lecturing me,' Aiden teased, and Zavier actually blushed. 'You've still never told me how much you had to offer to sway this divine creature.'

Laughing, Tabitha left them to it. After changing Darcy's nappy she pulled on his blue Babygro, admiring his little fat legs as he kicked happily in the air. He really was the most delightful baby, and of course that had nothing to do with his having two of the most biased parents. Gently placing him in his crib, Tabitha stood watching as he rolled onto his stomach, his fat bottom sticking up in the air as he searched for his thumb.

'Is he asleep?' Zavier asked as he crept in behind her.

'He's gone straight onto his stomach. Maybe I should turn him.'

'He'll only roll straight back.' Seeing her tense, Zavier grinned. 'Here.' She watched as his strong hand gently rolled the sleeping baby onto his back, never failing to marvel at how gentle and patient he was with his son. 'He's exhausted. It's been a great day.'

'Fantastic,' Tabitha agreed, nestling against his chest as they admired their sleeping baby. 'Your dad was so proud, and did you see the smile on my grandmother's face?'

'She's looking really happy. Bruce must be good for her—at least she's not gambling now. Mind you, they play a mean game of snap; I've never seen such concentration! I doubt Mum will pull the cards out next time they come for dinner. Anyway, enough about everyone else—there's something for you downstairs.'

'But we opened all the presents,' Tabitha said as she walked behind him. 'What's this?'

'It's for you. Open it.' His voice had gone strangely thick, and he couldn't quite meet her eyes as she snapped open the large velvet box he handed her.

'Oh, Zavier, it's stunning.' It was, too—a delicate neck chain, littered with rubies all different sizes. 'There must be hundreds here.'

'Forty,' Zavier said gruffly. 'One for each year of marriage. It's the one my grandfather had made for my grandmother for their fortieth anniversary.'

'Shouldn't you be doing this in thirty-nine years?' She watched the tiniest frown on his face. 'I'll still be around, Zavier. I'm not going anywhere; this is for keeps.'

'I know.' The frown vanished and his eyes lifted to hers. 'I guess I just want to keep hearing it—anyway, it seems a shame to have something so beautiful locked away when you could be wearing it.'

He fastened it tenderly around her neck and followed her to the large mirror over the fireplace.

'I can't believe I nearly let you go.'

'Don't.' Leaning against him, she closed her eyes, chasing away the nightmare of what could have been.

A world without Zavier.

'Can I ask you something?'

'Ask away,' he mumbled, only half listening as he pulled back the wild red curls, exposing the hollow of her shoulder on which he rained tiny kisses.

'Why don't you sell the business? Your parents are fine, I've got my dance school and Aiden's got his little gallery; what about taking the time to chase your dreams now?'

'What dreams?' He was working his way along her

collarbone, peeling back the thin strap of her dress with his teeth as his fingers worked their magic on her yielding breasts.

'Your dreams.' Tabitha forced her mind onto the one-sided conversation, determined to see it through. 'The ones you spoke about the night we got engaged.'

'I don't remember much talking. In fact all I can remember is this.' His hand was creeping down now, her dress slithering over her softly rounded bottom.

'The night we *first* got engaged, you said you had dreams…'

'Oh, that night.' In one easy motion he scooped her up, carrying her across the hall to the bedroom door, which he kicked impatiently open. 'You talk too much.'

'I'm serious, Zavier. I need to know if your dreams…'

'Chased, caught and fulfilled. Does that answer your question?'

'Honestly?'

Laying her on the bed, he slid down the last tiny remnant of her clothing before adding softly, 'Beyond my wildest expectations…'

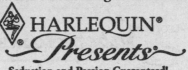

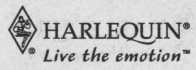

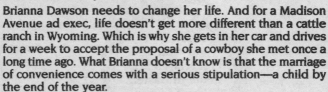
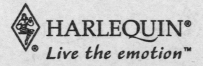

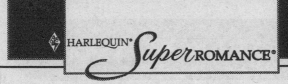

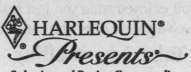

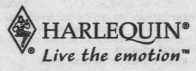

If you enjoyed what you just read,
then we've got an offer you can't resist!

Take 2 bestselling love stories FREE!

Plus get a FREE surprise gift!

Clip this page and mail it to Harlequin Reader Service®

IN U.S.A.	**IN CANADA**
3010 Walden Ave.	P.O. Box 609
P.O. Box 1867	Fort Erie, Ontario
Buffalo, N.Y. 14240-1867	L2A 5X3

YES! Please send me 2 free Harlequin Presents® novels and my free surprise gift. After receiving them, if I don't wish to receive anymore, I can return the shipping statement marked cancel. If I don't cancel, I will receive 6 brand-new novels every month, before they're available in stores! In the U.S.A., bill me at the bargain price of $3.57 plus 25¢ shipping & handling per book and applicable sales tax, if any*. In Canada, bill me at the bargain price of $4.24 plus 25¢ shipping & handling per book and applicable taxes**. That's the complete price and a savings of at least 10% off the cover prices—what a great deal! I understand that accepting the 2 free books and gift places me under no obligation ever to buy any books. I can always return a shipment and cancel at any time. Even if I never buy another book from Harlequin, the 2 free books and gift are mine to keep forever.

106 HDN DNTZ
306 HDN DNT2

Name	(PLEASE PRINT)	
Address	Apt.#	
City	State/Prov.	Zip/Postal Code

* Terms and prices subject to change without notice. Sales tax applicable in N.Y.
** Canadian residents will be charged applicable provincial taxes and GST.
  All orders subject to approval. Offer limited to one per household and not valid to current Harlequin Presents® subscribers.
  ® are registered trademarks of Harlequin Enterprises Limited.

PRES02   ©2001 Harlequin Enterprises Limited

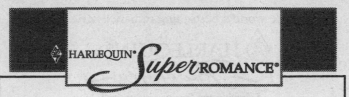

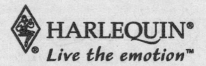

The world's bestselling romance series.

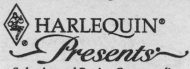

HARLEQUIN®
Presents

Seduction and Passion Guaranteed!

A gripping, sexy new trilogy from

Miranda Lee

THREE RICH MEN...

Three Australian billionaires—they can have anything, anyone...except three beautiful women....

Meet Charles, Rico and Ali, three incredibly wealthy friends all living in Sydney, Australia. Up until now, no single woman has ever managed to pin down the elusive, exclusive and eminently eligible bachelors. But that's about to change, when they fall for three gorgeous girls....

But will these three rich men marry for love— or are they desired for their money...?

Find out in Harlequin Presents®

A RICH MAN'S REVENGE—Charles's story
#2349 October 2003

MISTRESS FOR A MONTH—Rico's story
#2361 December 2003

SOLD TO THE SHEIKH—Ali's story
#2374 February 2004

Available wherever Harlequin® books are sold

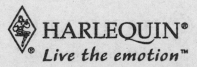

HARLEQUIN®
Live the emotion™

Visit us at www.eHarlequin.com

HSR3RM2